Scorn Twice

So Now What?

FATIMA CLEMENT

SCORN TWICE
SO NOW WHAT?

iUniverse books may be ordered through booksellers or by contacting:

iUniverse
1663 Liberty Drive
Bloomington, IN 47403
www.iuniverse.com
844-349-9409

ISBN: 978-1-6632-4759-9 (sc)
ISBN: 978-1-6632-4760-5 (hc)
ISBN: 978-1-6632-4761-2 (e)

Print information available on the last page.

iUniverse rev. date: 11/09/2022

This book is to inspire everyone young woman to focus on the future and allow their past to teach them a lesson to make them a better person in near future. I hope and pray many of us can relate to some of the obstacles in this great book.

INTRODUCTION

Tracee realizes that life is truly what you make it out to be. She will make you laugh and cry. Find out how her marriage is put to the ultimate test. Money, power, and respect don't make it easy for this young, up-and-coming entrepreneur—or does it? Every decision is not always the right decision.

She encounters so many obstacles that she feels like her life is turning out the way she had predicted it would. She has to make changes, and as you follow along, you will be able to relate to her situations. Does Tracee make it or break it? You decide!

ACKNOWLEDGEMENTS

Special thanks to my husband, Anthony. I know you were waiting very patiently for me to finish my book and loving all of *me!* I would also like to send a special thank you to the following people: my mom and dad; Tyesha, who is always watching my back; and Rockel. Well, Fam-Bam, this only the beginning. There will be plenty of more books to come. Also, I apologize for the swearing, but it allows me to get into character, so if I offended any one, I didn't mean to! Amen! Amen!

Fatima

xoxoxo

CHAPTER 1

Welcome to the Hood

I WAS ABOUT TO TURN SIXTEEN AND HAD JUST STARTED TO "smell my own ass," as grown folks would say. It was a hot summer day, and there was nothing to do, as usual. One of my homegirls from school decided to take me out and do some real shit. We went to what they call "Soul Skate" on Sunday nights. Well, to me that was like the only good thang going. We would go see some of the hottest moves on skates and see the new boys that would be out. If you were anybody or somebody, that was the place to be. Girls with the big old butts and the long-hair divas were amongst us hood girls.

They couldn't fuck with us 'cause when we would step out, it was on and poppin'. Bitches could not stand me and my girls. Oh, by the way, my name is Tracee. I live with my mom, Marie, and my little sister named Harmony in a middle-class neighborhood.

My two best friends are Aries and Tiny. One late night, after going skating, Tiny's cousin was trying to get at me. I was, like, cool 'cause I was on the rebound anyway. I was, like, "Who is your cousin? He is cute."

"His name is Walter, and I think you guys might hit it off."

Aries wanted to go kick it with him and his homeboys, and I said, "Fuck it; let's go." We were, like, four deep in Aries' car. We finally got to Tiny's cousin's apartment, and he had a house full of his college friends. Did I forget to mention that he was a college man? Well, now you know. As we got out of the car, I had to admit that I was a little nervous from the very beginning about going.

Basically, it was supposed to go down like this: everybody was supposed to hook up with someone at Walter's house. Of course, everyone didn't. There was a lot of clashing going on that night—men were trying to date young women and so forth. The few of us did actually hook up, and that was that. After we exchanged numbers, I decided to go on a date with Walter. By the time we set a date, he was on his way back to college. He was only home for the weekend, and so I told him that once he was back for the holidays, we would be able to get together.

The next time I saw Walter was when the county fair was in town. We went on our first date. I had to admit that he was the perfect gentlemen that night. He wasn't much of an amusement rider, so all we did was eat. We ate so much that I ended up getting a stomachache. He felt sorry for me, so he took me to get something for my pain. Walter was only in town for that weekend, and it turned out to be a great weekend for me. We began to write each other. I didn't have a lot of money, so a letter was cheaper than a phone call—I spoke to him once I got a calling card. Before I knew it, a whole two months had gone by.

Walter was going to a big university at the time. I often asked how he was able to find time for me and his studies. We made a promise to each other that when he got back, we would try to begin a steady relationship. As soon as Walter got back, we met each other's family. His grandmother and grandfather had raised him. I met several of his aunts, uncles, and cousins. To my surprise, Walter was related to a girl in my high school who didn't like me. I really wasn't worried about her, but I told Walter that she didn't like me. He said that he would work on that.

Kasha, Walter's cousin, approached me one day at school and said, "I know you told my cousin that I don't like you!" I looked her straight in the eye and said, "Yes, I sure did." All of a sudden, old country-ass Tiny walked up on the both of us. She had a funny look on her face. I said, "Why do you have an ugly frown on your face?" She replied, "My stupid jealous-acting cousin." I found out that Kasha had a crush on a guy that I used to go out with. All this came from her liking him, and I was supposed to have taken him from her. "Bitch, I didn't even know you knew him like that. As far as I was concerned, he apparently didn't notice you anyway." I told Kasha that I was not the only girl who was dating him at that time, and I was hurt about it. I also told her, "Don't be mad at me for dating someone that I didn't know you were interested in anyway." I told her that he was playing me and not to waste her time trying to hook up with him. About a week later she came to me and invited me to eat dinner with her and her mom. We became friends, and Tiny was very happy for the both of us.

I could now consider her a buddy or, shall I say, a friend. I was glad we became friends because I would not feel comfortable being around Walter when one of his family members did not like me. By this time Walter had asked me to be his girlfriend. He told me that he had never been serious about a girl before me.

I was, like, wow! I asked him, "Why me?" He said, "I like you a lot, and you're special." Everybody in his family was excited for us to be a couple. Aries, with her hot ass, was telling me to be aware of what comes with being with a college man. I was

3

looking at her like she was crazy. She says to me, "Don't act like this shit is new to you." I replied, "All men don't always want that right away."

She started laughing and then stopped. I asked her what the problem was. She said, "Look, you have been through a tough relationship already, and I'm trying to make sure that this is really what you want."

I was ready. Shit, I had never dated a man who was in college, let alone four years older than me. Aries had a lot of experience with guys, if you catch my drift. I understood what she meant about what comes with the territory of dating an older man. I was ready because my virginity was taken from me, and I knew that sex would be a factor in this new relationship. Aries told me, "Just be careful because you don't know if you're the only girl for him." Our relationship took off, new and exciting.

I was the envy of all the high school females. They were trying to figure out how the hell I got Walter. I found out later in our relationship that he had been the popular guy on our school campus, way before I started going there. He wasn't much of a ladies' man, so some say. Well, that wasn't my concern about what he was in the past, just how he treated me now in this relationship. It sound like a lot more jealousy was coming out than anything.

I wasn't worried about the rumors of his messing with another girl at my school. He made it perfectly clear that I was "the one." Dating Walter had its advantages. I had so much status as his girl that anywhere I went, I was treated like royalty. There wasn't anything a friend of his or a family member wouldn't do for me. If I needed a ride to school, they were there to pick me up.

Once people in the hood found out we were a couple, they even offered protection for me. I was a very popular girl, not to mention that I was a teen model in our state. I was one of the few in my class voted most likely to succeed in life. I knew I would be a handful for any man after the rebirth of the new me. I was so eager to be the best at everything I touched that there was no limit to what I could do. I had it all: popularity, envy, a college man, respect—oh, and don't forget brains.

I knew it was definitely time to get my shit together. I was ready to take on the role as his new "boo"! On a cloudy old Wednesday, I got a call from Walter's uncle Charlie. He asked me if I would like to surprise his nephew at school. I only knew a few of his relatives at the time, so I felt comfortable with his uncle Charlie paying for my plane ticket. All I had to do was figure out how I was going to go without getting busted by my mom.

Aries' mom was a flight attendant, and she was never home. I stayed a lot at her house from time to time, so she was the perfect alibi for me. The plan was that I was going to stay the weekend at Aries' house and that I would be back home on Monday after school, as usual. For some reason, my mom wasn't buying it. Aries had her mom call my mom to see if it was okay for me to spend the weekend with her, but my mom did not know that Mrs. Carmichael was going to be gone the whole week.

My perfect getaway was coming into play. I arranged for my ticket to be purchased and off I went. I was going to see my man. Nothing could possibly stop me now. When I got to California State University, I was greeted by some of Walter's homeboys who knew that I was coming. They were to keep Walter out of the apartment until I arrived. He had some good friends. I was happy that they were willing to see their homey be happy.

I called Aries, and she said, "Hey, don't forget to call your mom first thing in the morning, like usual." I told her okay and that I would see her when I got back. An hour later, I heard a voice—it was Walter. He had this look on his face like he had seen a ghost. I said hello, and he started grinning. He ran up to me and said, "What are you doing here, baby?"

I told him that Uncle Charlie had sent me to see him. He called his uncle and told him thank-you. I asked him what he wanted to do this weekend. He said, "Well, I'm going to show you off to the rest of my friends." I was, like, "Cool." He had a friend who was going into the NFL draft that year, and he really wanted me to meet him. He was very nice. His name was Tommy LaStrappe, and he was six foot three and weighed 265 pounds. I looked at him, and I was determined to see what animal he'd eaten. He was very muscular and had a beautiful smile. He asked me if I had a twin, and I said, "Yeah, but she is back at home." He said, "Home? Where is home?" I said that home was Las Vegas. Tommy said that he had never been to Las Vegas but if he ever went there, could he look up my sister? I told him, "Yeah, but she really isn't my sister. She's my best friend." He said, "Cool. I'll keep in touch with Walter and maybe if I'm in town, we all can get together."

I told him that was fine with me and wished him good luck. We left Tommy's apartment and went to a mall. Walter wanted to get me some shoes and an outfit. I was so excited. I wanted to see how much he was going to spend that evening. I got a pair of Jordan shoes and a shirt. We got matching shoes and shirts.

I asked him if he would like to take pictures to remember this lovely event. We made an appointment to have the pictures taken the very next day. Back then, that was what we did to show our appreciation for one another.

Also, it was proof that he was mine. I decided that on the way back to his apartment that I would have sex with him. I'd come all that way, and I wanted it to be special. While we were at the mall, I picked up some candles and when we got back to his apartment, I was so ready. I told him to run some bath water and that we would both get in it together. He looked at me like he wanted to eat me alive. Walter began to do what I asked him to do; then he stopped. I said, "What's wrong?" He said, "I don't want this to be a pressure-type weekend."

I told him it wasn't, and this is what I wanted. He went back into the bathroom and ran our bath water. I went in to test the temperature of the water. I knew it had to be the perfect evening so that we would both remember it.

I lit the candles around the tub and turned down the lights. Walter was a big Al Green fan. I put on some Al, and we got into the bathtub—I got in first, and he followed. He sat in between my legs. I wrapped them around him, and I began to squeeze the soaking wet towel all over his chocolate body. I was ready for whatever he wanted to do. I washed his body, and he washed mine. This felt *so good!* I acted like I was a pro in the bathtub. I saw this on an HBO special. I felt like there wasn't anything that could go wrong. We got out of the tub, and he wrapped a towel around my body and took me into his bedroom. We started kissing, and then ... I don't think I need to explain anything else. He was great. I lay there, enjoying every moment and minute of it.

Walter was very sexual, and he wanted to try different positions that I didn't know about. I wasn't experienced in sex yet. Walter was the second guy that I'd had sex with. He did things to me that I knew I would never forget. After we finished, I looked at the clock; it had lasted forty-five minutes.

I didn't know if that was good or bad, but I didn't give a fuck! It felt like it was longer than that. I rolled over with a big grin on my face. All I heard him do was breath heavy for about ten minutes. He said, "Don't get too comfortable because round two will begin very shortly."

My eyes got as big as a Dunkin' Donut hole. "Round two," I replied. He said, "Yeah. You thought that was it for the night." I said, "Yeah," and he said, "Hell, no! I won't get any ass from you for about three more weeks, and you expect me to not take advantage of your sexy body right now?" I lay there with this crazy look on my face. Then, about fifteen minutes later, it was on again. Walter was controlling every ounce of my 115-pound frame.

I didn't stop him at all. He knew what to do to me, and everything he did was great. I was so tired after round two that I fell fast asleep. He fell asleep, too. The next morning I was awakened by the smell of bacon, eggs, and toast. Walter got up and made me breakfast in bed. I was so happy! He made sure a girl could never forget this. After breakfast he wanted some morning sex, and honey, I gave it to him. My cookie was so swollen that after we did it, I had to go soak in the tub for about thirty minutes. Walter took a shower and got himself ready, and so I began to get myself ready. All of a sudden, Aries called Walter's phone. I answered it, and she screamed, "Did you call your mom yet?" I was like, "No, but stay on the phone and put it on mute, so that if she has any questions I can make it seem like you picked up the other phone in the house." The plan worked, and I told Aries I owed her one. Walter and I left to go take our pictures and eat dinner.

Walter wanted to go back to his apartment so he could do some homework. I was a little tired anyway, so I was also ready to go back too. We got back, and I took a long nap. Walter sat at his computer, working, and didn't here me come into the living room. I had on his T-shirt, and he had on nothing. I looked at him ... and you know the rest!

Walter gave me the best weekend ever. I had so much to tell Aries when I got back that I knew she would trip out. Aries was a pro at getting niggas to do stuff for her, and she wasn't afraid to give it up. I knew that I didn't want to follow in her footsteps. She did what she did to get what she wanted, but I did the opposite. Aries and I had a complete understanding about each other. She didn't step on my toes, and I didn't step on hers.

We had a friendship that most people could relate to. Aries' dad was an engineer for the government, so she never really had a father-and-daughter relationship with her dad. All she got was gifts and phone calls from him, so I began to think she treated guys like she did because of how her dad treated her. Her mother didn't mind too much because she did her own thing most of the time anyway.

I was really Aries' comfort, and the fact that her family had money didn't do them any justice at all. We looked out for one another all the time, so when I told her that I wanted to go see Walter, she was excited for me. The weekend ended faster than

I could remember. All we did was eat and have sex all day on Sunday. I didn't want it to end, but I did have to get back home and back to reality. Walter seemed sad when he had to take me to the airport.

We cuddled for about an hour and for the rest of the evening, we talked about what we were going to do when he got back home. Of course, first things first: my quality time with him. I waited so impatiently for him to get back to Vegas. We went out with some of his family for dinner.

At the time, the state fair was going on in the city. I asked him to take me and that was our very first in-state picture together. We were like a match made in heaven. I was his, and he was mine. Aries always said that I would know if I truly cared about a person. She said you get these funny feelings when you are around that special someone. I can recall several occasions when we were together, and I had bubbles in my stomach. Walter was the "it" guy, and yes, *bitches*, I have him all to myself. Walter decided that he needed to be back home with his family and, of course, with me. I really didn't know what was in store for our relationship.

I was just happy to have him home for the week—we were inseparable. When he was home, he took me to and from school and home every day. My mom was very impressed about Walter. He managed to have an apartment and go to school full time. Like I said, being with him had its rewards.

He took very good care of me. I never asked for anything, and if I needed anything, he made sure that I got it. His whole family loved me, but nothing could prepare me for what Aries found out after Walter got settled back home.

Aries was like my protector at times. I knew she would never turn on me, and I would never turn on her. When she decided to call me at Walter's house, I was very pissed off. She told me that she'd found out that he was gang-affiliated. That explained why I never got approached by other men, and if I did and I told them who I was dating, they would walk away. I never thought anything of it, to be honest. I just thought that Walter was popular. I never knew his past and what other family members had done to give him such a status to carry on. Shit, I felt like I was dating Al Capone or something. I felt like he was Clyde, but I didn't want to be Bonnie. I decided to ask him about his family hush-hush members. He decided to tell all.

He began to tell me about his on-the-run cousins, kill-at-first-sight cousins, bank-robber uncles, and beat-a-girl-down aunts, not to mention his pimping brothers and car-jacking cousins. He also told me about how his family had bad karma.

Death was a part of his entire upbringing. After hearing all the stories behind his family members, I thought about what the hell I was doing with this man. None of this mattered to me, though—it wasn't him; it was his family, and I didn't care. None of these members could affect our relationship ... or so I thought. The more I went around them, the more I could feel the karma in the air.

Aries thought that I would break up with him after hearing all the horror stories. All it did was make me more curious about how a man so fine didn't have girlfriends and committed relationships. It just made me get closer to him. I had a real bad boy, and bad boys drove bad cars. I can say he always made me feel safe. We argued a lot. We made up also.

Walter never liked to end his day with the both of us being mad at each other. So, who cares? Sometimes fussing made us more aware of each other's feelings, and sometimes I felt like we needed to yell. He also was very controlling. It wasn't so noticeable at the beginning of the relationship. Farther into the months—exactly six months down the road—was when I noticed how insecure he really was about being together.

After all, I was his first real committed relationship, and I guess I should have been more alert. This was all brand new for him; it wasn't for me. We got real close; then one day, he decided to pull what we call a "ho card." This fool tried to set me up. Everything was going good. He called me and said, "Can I meet you at the park so we can have a face-to-face talk with one another?"

I said, "Cool, I'll be there." When I got there, he had a strange look on his face. It was something I had never seen before. I asked him what was up and why he needed to meet with me. This is why you keep your friends close and your enemies closer. Some girl had told him that I was cheating on him. I frowned at him and said, "Where is this coming from? Who in the hell told you that? Furthermore, why you are listening to some girl who I don't even know?" He looked at me and said, "Maybe all this is too much for the both of us right now." I began to cry. I could not believe this. He was breaking up with me.

I couldn't believe this was really happening! He offered to take me home, but luckily, Aries' house was across the park's field. I told him not to bother; that I would walk to Aries' house. I cried for about three hours, and Aries was pissed off. She couldn't believe it herself—all over some "he says/she says" bull crap. I was with Walter for a year, and I was more in shock about his listening to some girl. Aries was trying to cheer me up. I was so mad at him. We broke up right when the damn summer was about to start.

I really could not think of any other reason for us to break up, unless he was trying to test the waters. I thought some little hot-to-trot girl had a little switch in her walk and just caught his attention. Instead of cheating on me, maybe he needed an excuse to break up with me. That was the only reason I could come up with for why Walter wanted to break up with me. I thought I had my game wrapped tight.

Aries wanted to go get into a little trouble that weekend, and I went with her. I was sad and missing Walter, but he wasn't thinking about me. I didn't even try to call him, nor did he call me. A month went by, and I decided to get my head right and go out to the club with Aries. On a hot sunny day, I got a voice mail on my home phone. Yep, it was Walter. He sounded so pitiful. I didn't even respond to his message. I pulled out my "fuck him, girl" booty shorts, and I was ready to catch me a new man. We were on the prowl, and nothing could stop this lioness in her sexy straps. As we arrived at the club that night, I saw some of Walter's friends' cars in the parking lot. Aries looked at me and said, "If you saw what I saw, then you know he will be up in here." I didn't care.

Whatever. As soon as we walked in, I was getting nothing but pure attention. I have to admit, I was looking good—fresh perm, glossy lips, clear skin, pocket full of money, bomb-ass outfit, *priceless*! Then, about twenty minutes into the club scene, I heard my name being called. "Tracee! Tracee! Ah, girl, I know you hear me." I looked to the left, then to my right. Huh! It was Walter. He approached me and began to rub on my legs.

I slapped his hands down and started to walk away. He tried to grab me, but my girlfriends were quicker than he was. "Can I talk to you?" he asked. I looked at him and said, "There is nothing to talk about, and you need to do you, boo! Just do you, boo!" Before the night was over I had so many phone numbers, I didn't know what to do with myself. Aries was ready to leave the club. I had so much fun. I really needed the girls night out on the town.

Walter began to blow up my damn phone all night long. I had so many messages from him, it was ridiculous. I started to go out on a date with a guy named Omar that I'd met in the club. He was really cute. He was older than me, and he played AAA baseball. We went on a date every day for two weeks straight. He liked to have fun and have no worries, and at that time, that was what I was looking for.

Omar was quiet, and he allowed me to take charge of our dates. He didn't even like to raise his voice. It was a very calm relationship. During the little time we were together, I was able to attend some of his games. It is very exciting to watch in person and then on TV. Omar said to me what Walter had said to me: "You are a very special kind of woman, and if any man can keep you happy, he would be happy, too."

I decided to return Walter's call after three weeks. He begged me to take him back, and I told him that I was seeing someone, and I wanted to get to know him a little more. Why did I say that to him? Walter came to my house so quick that I couldn't even explain what I wanted to do. He came over, and that was when

I knew he was crazy. He made me get into his lowrider, and we fought the whole ride back to his house.

I was screaming and slapping him all in his face. He snatched me up into his house, and we began to cuss each other out. I got so mad that I broke whatever I could in the house. He threatened me so many times, but I knew he wouldn't harm me at all. That mutha-fucka slapped the shit out of me.

I was in shock. He slapped me so hard, I didn't know if I should cry or slap him back. He grabbed me and threatened to hurt me really bad if I didn't get back with him. I told him to promise not to hit me again, and I would think about getting back with him. I should have known then that later he would become very possessive with me. I agreed to let bygones be bygones. He, of course, wanted to have sex. I hadn't had any, so of course I gave it up to him.

Walter had a wedding to go to in California, and I told him that when he got back, we could sit down and have a real talk about our relationship. He took me home afterwards, and I was content.

I liked Omar so much that I told him whatever he wanted to hear so that I could get back to my house. Omar called me so much that I couldn't get any more voice mails that day. I called him back, and we instantly became a couple. When Walter got back from the wedding, I had to tell him that I was seeing someone, and he went crazy. He started talking about beating up Omar, but he didn't even know him. He also said that Omar wasn't the right man for me and that I would never find anyone better than him.

I dated Omar for about four months. Our entire short relationship had interruptions from Walter, until Omar decided it was too much for him. Omar and I agreed that we would remain friends, and if I ever needed him, he would always be there for me. Basically, we broke up, and I decided to go back to Walter.

I have to admit that we were very happy again for about the first three months. I asked Walter why he'd believed the rumor, and he said he hadn't; it was a test to see if he really wanted to be with me.

I told him that it was ugly, the way he went about it. I told him never to do that again, and he vowed he never would try that again. I told him that the only way we would ever have a good, strong relationship was if we talked it out instead of yelling and fighting. We both agreed. I called Aries to update her on all that had gone on, and she was in shock about everything. She said, "Both of y'all are meant for each other because y'all is crazy-ass people." Like she could talk. Even my sister Harmony was tripping off of Walter and me getting back together. She said she thought that we were done with each other, too. Harmony and her opinion is a trip. As long as I didn't tell her that he slapped me, she would not tell our mom what was going on and also reveal all my dirty little secrets. I loved her for being there for me, and she also knew that I would be there for her. I really couldn't explain why I went back to Walter, but I really wasn't ready for what was about to happen next.

I went to visit Walter one last time in California. I had a different vibe when I flew out this time. He was happy to see me, but I had mixed feelings. In fact, I was thinking about Omar. Something strange had come over me during my flight into town.

I looked at Walter differently; I couldn't explain it. I noticed he did a little redecorating. He got a new king-sized leather headboard, caramel colored to be exact. It came with matching dresser and mirror. I told him it was nice and that a little change was good for him. He was kind of a "plain Jane" when it came to decorating. He said that he was doing it for me. How exciting! I love when I have an effect on people and that how some things matter more to others.

I was just preparing myself for anything and everything. I had a lot to think about, but Omar was always on my mind. Heavy. Too heavy.

CHAPTER 2

Why Did She Go and Do That?

WHEN I ARRIVED BACK IN LAS VEGAS, ARIES WAS waiting for me at baggage claim. She acted like she hadn't seen me in years. I'd missed her, too. She wanted to know everything that had happened between me and Walter. I told her everything, every detail, not leaving out anything.

I also told her I had someone that she would meet when he came to the city. She was all excited, and she knew he had to be cute because she knew I wouldn't waste her time. I told her he was going up for NFL draft, and she wanted to know who he was. I told her he was nice, his name was Tommy LaStrappe, and he was six foot three and weighed 265 pounds.

I also told her that he had a nice body and that I would introduce them soon. Aries took me home, and I acted like nothing happened. My little sister Harmony was all in my business. She loved to remind me that we were only a year apart in age and that she knew what I was up to. I had something on her, so she could never tell on me because she knew if Mom found out, she would be devastated. I had a long talk with Harmony to update her on my new Walter.

She wanted to see Walter and thank him for taking care of me that weekend. I told her that he was coming with a friend of his, and she was cool with it. I often wonder if she was sexually active but I figured she would tell me when she was ready. I know she talked to boys on the phone a lot. Harmony had this innocent look and that is probably why she could get away with a lot of stuff.

Harmony was about five foot seven and weighed about 125 pounds—tall for her age and very thin. The funny thing was that she had a big butt. She didn't look sixteen, either. We were born on the same day but a year apart. My mom couldn't have done anything worse to the both of us. We really don't look that much alike, considering we have the same dad.

Harmony took after our dad with her height, and I got his green eyes and our mother's height. Did I forget to tell you about my green eyes? Sorry, if I did. I tried to spend an equal amount of time with Harmony and Aries. I told her that Walter might be the man I would have kids with. Harmony wanted to get to know Walter a little better before we began to breed some babies. I wasn't mad for her putting it out there about her request. I told her everything, just in case something was to happen to me. Harmony knew that I liked Walter a lot. She was worried that Walter would take me from her, and she was not having that.

She was already mad that she shared me with Aries. She wasn't about to let Walter in that easily. I told her that she and Walter should get together and have a talk about me and what she expected from him as a man for big sister. If you knew Harmony, believe me, you'd know that she would do just that. Walter was coming home, and he told me that he would bring Tommy home with him.

Three weeks passed by so quickly. As a man of his word, Tommy came back with Walter. As soon as Walter got into town, he called me right away. I told him that my little sister wanted to talk to him before we left. He came right over, and my mom got a chance to meet Tommy. Harmony asked Walter so many questions that I thought she had run him off.

After completing her third-degree questions, she told him she was through asking, and he was all right with her. He smiled at me and gave everybody a hug and told them we were leaving. I told him to hold up a second so I could find out where Aries' hot tail was. Aries, being the spoiled brat that she is, was out getting her nails done. I told her we were on our way to meet up with her. Aries was so thrilled to meet Tommy.

We went on a date together to see if Aries and Tommy would hit it off. Aries loved to flirt and had no problem hiding it. Tommy and Aries got into a serious conversation at the table, and Walter and I didn't know if we needed to leave or what. It was heated at the table. I asked Aries to join me in the ladies room, but she said nah. I was very surprised to hear her say that to me, and Walter got upset. He caught on quickly and asked Tommy to meet him at the bar for a quick drink, but Tommy said, "Hell, no." Walter and I were now both pissed off. I was so ready to go. Aries began to sob and Tommy came to the rescue. We paid for dinner, and Walter and I said our good-byes, and Aries and Tommy left together. I was trying to figure out what this was in Aries' plan to see what kind of a man Tommy would be. That tramp! I said the bitch was good, and she knew how to get men to do what she wanted them to do. I guess I got to see the shit for myself.

I began laughing, and I was through with her for the evening. Walter took me to see some of his family, and they were excited to see us together. Later that evening we went to the park, and I wanted to give him a good-bye gift. We went to a bench, and

I made him unbutton his jeans. I did what any young woman would do in the heat of the moment: I jumped on top of him and rode him like a horse. Well, giddy-up, giddy-up, giddy-mutha-fucking-up! Walter just moaned and moaned for about fifteen minutes. All he could do was squeeze my butt. I loved it! It was risky, and I'm a risk-taker. I wanted to show him that I didn't care if anyone saw what we were doing. He apparently didn't care. When we finished, we went back to Aries' house, but there was no answer. I got worried, so I called her cell phone. She called me right back. I told her we had come to her house, but there was no answer at her door. She said that she and Tommy had gone to the grocery store to get popcorn for the movies they had rented. They wanted to know if we wanted to watch the movies with them, and of course we did. They rented a scary movie so we could cuddle up under them. Whatever. Y'all ain't slick. We knew what was up.

Aries pulled me into her bedroom and told me she was going to have sex with Tommy. I told her she was moving too fast. Aries really don't like criticism on what decisions she may make. I felt that it was too soon to get to know a guy, but only she could decide what was right. The movie started off boring, but then it got real interesting. We watched about an hour of the movie and began to get very sleepy. I dozed off and so did Walter. When I woke up, it was about 2:30 AM. I woke Walter, but we couldn't find Aries or Tommy. I knew what was going on. Aries' house was huge. They had about seven bedrooms. I had my own room at her house. Walter and I went to bed.

The next morning Aries came into my room and started jumping on the bed. I told her that she was goofy and had too much energy for me in the morning.

Walter asked, "Where is Tommy?"

"He's downstairs cooking us some breakfast."

Tommy could cook. He'd taken a culinary arts class at school. They had a lot in common because Aries took the same class at our high school. I couldn't wait to get Aries' hot tail alone so that I could ask her about her night with Tommy. I knew she cut up real bad. After we all sat down for breakfast, we talked about people in our lives. I really didn't know if Aries and Tommy would try to have a relationship after the night they'd had, but we would soon find out.

Walter gave me a kiss, and we said our good-byes. Aries walked over to Tommy, and they exchanged phone numbers and addresses. Off they went. I went to take shower to relax my body. I then called my mom to tell her that I would be home in a couple hours. I got dressed and went into Aries' bedroom. Before I could ask her what had happened between her and Tommy, she began to tell me herself.

I was in shock to find out what they did the whole night. Aries told me she took her clothes off and then lay on the bed. She said she looked at him, as if waiting for him to do what any man would do in a situation when it was presented. To her surprise, he told her that this was not what he had come for; he asked if she'd mind if they cuddled all night.

I know Aries was tripping on the inside because I was sitting on the edge of the bed with my damn mouth wide open in shock. I guess she was cool with it. I asked her if it had bothered her that he didn't want to get in bed with her. She told me no not really. *Whatever!* We talked about what kind of gentlemen he was and then discussed the whole weekend. After that, I went home. It was time to go mess with my little sister. I knew she was missing her big sister. Harmony is a trip.

She wanted to know to what went on between them. I basically told what I knew. She wasn't impressed with the outcome. I told her that some men are dogs, and some are not. Harmony wasn't shy at all. I told her that when she decided to go on a date that Aries and I would be right there for her. She looked at me and said, "Uh, no, thank you!" I wanted to say that my feelings were very hurt, and so I told her. She said, "I don't need one and two watching how I make my moves on my date." I also forgot that she thought she was grown, too.

As time went on, Walter kept telling me that he missed me a lot. I asked him when was he coming back home, and he said, "Soon, baby." I noticed that this particular night of lovemaking was different.

I woke up in a lazy mood. Aries and Harmony noticed that my body language was different. My sleep habits were changing and my "little friend" had not shown up that month. We went to go get a pregnancy test from Walgreen's. It was positive.

I took another test. It was positive, too. Little did I know that the day when Walter and I had sex, we had made a baby? Yep, I was pregnant. I was very scared. I didn't know what to do. I called Walter and asked him to come home because I had something to share with him.

"Is it bad news?" he asked.

"No, but I won't tell you until you get here."

I had to wait about three or four weeks before he came home and I told him the news. Wow! He was in shock! Then he gave me the most comforting hug and said, "It will be okay, baby.

I'll make sure everything will be better for all three of us!" I'd thought he was going to be mad, but he accepted it right away. He even told me that he knew I was pregnant because he was eating all kinds of foods.

I wasn't eating like that. He was excited and ready to tell the whole damn world. Now, don't forget I was only seventeen years old—a few weeks shy of my eighteenth birthday. I had to figure out how the hell I was going to tell my mom. Unfortunately, as months went by, I couldn't bear to tell my mother. I told Harmony, and she told Ruby, one of our dad's sisters. We called her "Aunt Special."

My grandmother had a name for all of her dysfunctional children. My aunt came over every day and asked if I wanted her to go with me to tell my mother. I wouldn't let her. When I finally decided to tell my mom, I was six months pregnant and was showing; I couldn't hide the big belly anymore.

I called my mom at work and told her that I had to talk to her as soon as possible. I went to Walter's house, and we both called her together. Mom was pissed off—I knew she would be. I was in love, and it really didn't matter to me what she thought of us having a baby. Walter's family accepted the fact that we were adding another member to their family. I hadn't forgotten that I was getting myself involved with a family that had a lot of negative karma in their lives.

During my pregnancy, two or three of Walter's family members passed away. I really wasn't good at funerals, so I didn't go to them. As my due date grew closer, I had a sit-down chat with Walter's grandmother. I asked why there was so much heartache in the family and deaths. Her real name was Josephine Pavilion, but everyone who knew her called her "Sweetie." Sweetie told me it all started when her children were young. Her identical twin sister, Jody, had kids at the same time as Sweetie, and soon, they had a total of nine kids each. Sweetie's parents had a total of seventeen children themselves—twins played a big part in her family life.

Sweetie said it would take a while to get me caught up with all the deaths. She looked me straight in my eyes and said, "I can't cry anymore, baby, I'm so tired. I will tell you my stories, and it is okay with me if you cry." I looked at Sweetie and smiled and then she began to talk.

It all began in the early 1970s when Afros and tight-ass jeans were the look! Sweetie told me about when she experienced her first death in the family. Her sister Jody's third child, a daughter named Billy, died of heart failure at the age of twenty-two. Billy was coming from the club with her older two sisters—they'd had so much fun—but when they arrived home, Billy passed out right in front of the house. They rushed her to the hospital, but she was pronounced dead on arrival. This was the first of many deaths that followed in the family. It seemed as if it was tick for tack. Sweetie said, "I really didn't think we could get through it, but we did." The following year, Sweetie's only son, David, was murdered by his best friend. He had been a painter and a track star. When I asked how he died, she said, "That boy killed my baby."

She had been in her backyard, raking leaves, when David said, "Hey, Mom, I'll be right back to help you clean up this backyard." She yelled, "Don't be gone too long because the sun is going down, and I don't want to do this in the damn dark!" He gave her a hug and a kiss and laughed, saying, "I'm going to Sherman's house to drop off some paintings to his mom. I'll be right back."

Sweetie looked up and said to her, "Every time those two boys get together, I know I won't see him for a while." About twenty-five minutes later she saw an ambulance speed past her house. No sooner did she get to the front of the house than she saw her daughter, Michelle, crying and saying, "Momma, Momma, oh, Momma."

Sweetie's eyes started pouring out tears and she screamed, "Please don't let it be David!" Michelle hated to tell her the bad news, but it was David. He had been stabbed to death by his best friend. After rushing him to the hospital, he had lost too much blood to save him—in fact, he had been stabbed so many times that when Sweetie arrived at the hospital, they didn't even want her to see him. She made a pact that next year that she would only clean her backyard while wearing her son's tennis shoes. She said she wore his tennis shoes to clean her yard for ten years until one day she took them off, washed them, them had then bronzed.

I can remember her telling me that he loved to do yard work. His paintings were all over the house, but his shoes were the only thing left that he had touched before he died. David died so young and tragically. He hadn't had a chance to have kids. Sweetie was a very strong black woman. I couldn't imagine how it would feel to lose my only son.

Sweetie's second oldest daughter, Hale, was raped, stabbed, and beaten to death about a year later. Hale was a hustler, and no one messed with her. She was that old saying, "A nigga ya love to hate" for real. Hale was sexy and strong-minded. She drove the men crazy. She knew how to get what she wanted without sleeping with the men she dealt with. "Pimping"—yep, that's what they called it. She was good and terrible at the same time. Hale never let people near her children, and she always took care of them. Hale would make the men she hung out with pay her bills and spend their money on her babies. Hale felt that with the lifestyle she lived, there was no room for commitment. Sweetie and Hale would fight about her getting a steady man in her life for the sake of the children. Hale felt like there was no time for that. You really couldn't tell her anything anyway. It was always her way or no way at all. I guess one man thought enough was enough. She died real young, too—her body was thrown on the side of the road. A passing car stopped to see what it was and discovered the badly beaten woman.

Hale had met her match. The man she'd been dating set her up, and one day she knew she would have to face those consequences. Hale knew that the lifestyle she'd chosen would catch up with her sooner or later.

Sweetie felt like her strength was being tested. She said that she felt there was nothing else that could go wrong in her life. When she arrived at the hospital, the doctor said that Hale was in a coma, and if she came out of the coma, she would be a vegetable. Sweetie's whole body went numb at hearing this news. She had to make one of the biggest decisions of her life.

The question was, "How does a mother decide whether to pull the plug or pay expensive medical bills to keep her comatose daughter alive?" Sweetie prayed and went to church. She felt that only God could help her with this decision. Well, she did what any mother would do: she waited and waited and waited, and then she decided, out of good faith, that it was time to let Hale go.

Sweetie had to get her mind right to take on a bigger challenge in her house—she had to make room for more kids. You would have thought she'd opened an orphanage. She had so many kids, but not enough bedrooms to hold all of them. Hale had three children that she left behind. Instead of splitting them up, Sweetie kept them all together.

I knew I wasn't ready to hear about the final tragedy, but I had to hear it anyway. Sweetie's oldest daughter, Yvette, was hanged and burned to death. Her husband had tried to kill her and all four of their children. He was drunk, and they had gotten into an argument over dinner. He left the house for several hours and came back to kill all of them. He filled the house with fuel and then lit the match to burn down the house. The oldest of the four children smelled the smoke first. He broke their bedroom window and started lifting the children out of the window. Escaping from flames, he went back into the house to get his mother and little sister, but suddenly the smoke got so bad that he was able to grab only his baby sister and scream for his mother to follow him out of the burning room.

Yvette yelled, "Get my babies out! I'm coming." As the two looked back to see if their mom was behind them, the ceiling fell down, and she was trapped behind the burning doors. The children all stood outside with scrapes and small burns on their arms and legs as they watched the house burn.

A neighbor called Sweetie and told her that Yvette's house was in flames and that she should get over there immediately. It was too late; Yvette had died in her bedroom. Her husband, Alfred, said, "I can't believe what I did to our family." He cried, "I'm sorry! I'm so sorry!" A week later, Alfred committed suicide.

Now, Sweetie had Hale's three children and Yvette's four children living with her.

I was so sad for her. Yes, this was the beginning stages of karma in their lives. The deaths started to slowly fade away for about ten years. It seemed as if one brother or sister had a tragedy; then it kept coming and coming. Every death in their family resulted in three or four new babies being born, including my son. I had a beautiful baby boy! He weighed 8 pounds 7 ounces. We named him Walter Lee Skillman Jr. This was the beginning of Walter's and my new family together. When Walter Jr. was a year old, Walter and I decided to get an apartment together. I felt that I needed to become more responsible for my actions by moving out of my mother's home.

Of course, we were new to being parents and living away from our families. I really didn't have much of a social life because I was a full-time mom and girlfriend. I noticed a change in Walter. I asked him, "Why are you so angry all the time?" Walter started to hang out with some guys I really didn't care too much for. He stayed out late and picked arguments with me. We fought so much that he started drinking a lot and then started smoking weed.

Now, I don't knock anyone's habit, but I'll be damned if he was going to be doing the shit around my baby. We argued, fussed, and sometimes even came to blows in the face about the dumb shit he was doing. I remember trying to leave him—I picked up Junior out of his crib, and Walter grabbed me and forced me to put Junior back in his crib so we could talk. Talking turned into yelling, and yelling turned into his pushing me through a bedroom window. All I could do was yell and kick at him. He told me, "You are not going anywhere unless I say so."

I was scared for my life after that. I was in a relationship that I now felt I needed to get out of. I felt like there was no respect for me. He wanted me to be his slave. This man was older than me, and he was showing a side of him that I didn't like.

He began to beat me at least three days a week. I was allowed to go to work and drive straight home. He timed my every move. He had me in total control. I really didn't like him so much. I felt like I couldn't turn to any of my friends. I had thoughts of suicide. Shit—murder, too! I cried to and from work. I knew that if someone found bruises on my body that they would call the police on Walter—and if that happened, then I would be safe from him.

This man was fucking crazy! I was out of my rabbit-ass mind to think that I would actually be safe with him. The reality was that I could only hope for the best. As usual, it turned out to be the worst. I had gotten to the point where I thought maybe he would just knock me out cold and I would never wake up. I thought maybe one time would be the final time. He was so much bigger than me. I felt that God needed to be more involved in my life. I knew that the only way God could be a part of my life was to pray, so praying became a much-needed part of my abusive life. I was getting sick and tired of him. I tried to find ways to make him happy. I cooked his breakfast. I came home for some afternoon sex. I even ran his happy-go-lucky ass some bath water. Nothing was good enough.

Walter always said to me, "When a woman starts to do nice things for her man, she is cheating on her man." I had this fucked-up look on my face. Hell, I was just trying to keep him from beating me, and all I did was start him up again.

Nothing worked with him. I tried to dress sexy and perform like a stripper, and he slapped me dead in my face. All I could do was cry. I was running out of tricks and seduction moves. I called my good old faithful sidekick Aries. I asked her to meet me at our favorite place to eat. This restaurant had the best tacos and burritos you could ever eat. It was called Gonzalez. People came from all over to eat there.

I had reserved a table for us. Aries walked in, but before she sat down, she grabbed my face and said, "I'm going to kill that bastard." I looked at her and told her what was going on in my life. She cried. She just couldn't believe that such a beautiful woman was putting up with this lifestyle.

I had to tell her everything, and all she could do was get mad. She asked me, "Do you want to leave him?" I paused, but before I could answer, I blacked out at the table.

When I woke up, Walter was standing over me and shouting! I thought for one second that I was having lunch with Aries. I got up off the floor and looked around. Startled and confused, I blinked about three times and realized this mutha-fucka had knocked me unconscious.

He was bolder than anybody. He hit me in public with people around. I started calling Aries' name, and she grabbed my hand and sat me on the bench. Shaking, she yelled, "Somebody please call the police!" Before I could put my hands over her mouth, I found a place of relief in my heart. I didn't know if I was happy or scared, but I didn't care at that time. I was finally about to get some peace in my life—at least, that's what I thought for a second or two.

CHAPTER 3

A Sista Cries for Help

HE SNATCHED MY ARM SO FAST AND WHISPERED IN MY EAR, "If you don't get you ass up, it will be problems." You would have thought that after the scene he had just caused that he would be scared, but he wasn't. This was just another trigger point in his mind. I sat with a dazed look on my face again. One part of my mind was telling me, *Get up! Get your ass up!* The other part of my mind was telling me, *Stay until the police arrive. This is your only freedom.* Now, what was a girl to do? I was sad and happy at the same time. I knew that if I went back to Walter that the beatings were going to get worse. I also knew that if I didn't go back and he later caught me alone, he would probably kill me.

I asked Aries if she could lend me some money to get a hotel room. I needed time to think about what my next move was going to be. I also had to make sure that I wasn't being followed. I needed time to put everything out on the table. I had to be certain that this is what I wanted to do. I had to make a decision about my life and my son. He didn't need to see this anymore. I knew if I went back that serious beatings would occur. I also knew that if I stayed away that I finally would have beat Walter at something for once. The only thing I hated was that he had everything—the money, clothes, cars all belonged to him. I didn't have anything in my name.

I did what any woman would do; I went to talk to Big Cousin, the oldest cousin in the family. For legal reasons we were not allowed to say his real name. I told him what was going on in my life; I told him I needed some protection—a nice, small handgun. He told me that if I got caught with the gun, I had better make up one good story on how I got the gun.

"These are not always used for protection," Big Cousin warned me. "They can kill if used in the wrong way."

I knew what was up. I knew what I was getting myself into. I wasn't worried at all. I called Aries and told her to meet me at her house. When she arrived, I made her get into my car. "What's up?" she asked. I told her my plan. She looked at me as if I was crazy, but I said that I needed to go back to the house of hell and get some of my and Junior's things.

Aries begged and pleaded with me not to go back.

"I got a gun," I said confidently, "and he doesn't want to make me do something that I might regret later." Years ago, I had written out my plan; now, I really needed Aries to read it over and tell me what she thought of it. My plan was as follows:

1. Get a gun.
2. Get a rental car from which to track Walter, day to day in a twenty-four-hour period.
3. Write down his every move.
4. Figure out the best time to go into the home.
5. Make sure I'm not followed.
6. Figure out how long it would take to run in and out.
7. Grab everything that we need.
8. DON'T FORGET THE MONEY!

I knew that this was going to take some time to prepare, but I was willing to risk everything to get it. I refused to let Walter beat me and drag me through the house by my hair. I was tired of his later begging for my forgiveness. No, no, no. I needed to clear my head and get it together. I was about to take a big step in my life, and I didn't have anybody to watch my back in case I needed an alibi. Walter wasn't ready for this ass-whipping that I was about to give him.

I contacted my old in-and-out-of-prison cousin, Pooky, to help me pull this off. Shit—I had to pay this fool, too. In order to help me commit to this outlandish beat-down, I knew Pooky would want some serious money. All I had to offer was about $10,000 in cash.

He needed a new life, and this would help him get on his way. We agreed that if something happened to either of us, we would not turn on one another. Pooky was a bit naïve, but I knew he wanted the money so bad. He knew what to do to get it from me.

The plan was ready; we went over and over it for about three weeks. I was so ready for Walter; I couldn't eat or sleep. My cousin Pooky refused to do the job before I had some rest. He told me I needed to eat and sleep because planning an attack took a lot of energy out of a person.

"I'm sorry," I said. "I will try to get some rest soon."

"If you don't rest for at least three or four days straight, I won't help you," Pooky insisted.

I agreed then to sleep. I decided to get all of my belongings from Walter on a Friday. Pooky felt that was a good day also.

We drew out our attack plans and did a run-through in case all else failed. I drove by the apartment and sat in my car for three hours, waiting on Walter to leave. I knew that once he left, I could put the plan in motion.

As soon as Walter left, I ran inside and grabbed my baby's clothes, diapers, and important papers. I ran back in the apartment a second time to grab my important documents, clothes, shoes— and oh, the money we had hidden for a rainy day.

I ran to the car and drove off like a mad woman. I didn't look back. I knew what I had done, and it was for my baby and my new life without Walter. I got about twenty minutes up the road and my cell phone starting ringing like crazy. I refused to answer it until I made it back to my hotel. and Pooky and I had unloaded everything from the car; then I answered my phone. It was Walter.

He called me everything from a bitch, to a whore, to a slut. All I could do was laugh at him.

I told him, "You will never get the chance to hurt me again. You will never get the chance to treat me like shit, either. I will see you in court. Don't call me anymore or try to find me."

My cousin Pooky felt it wouldn't be safe for me to be in the hotel by myself so he vowed to stay with me until I got back on my feet. I was so happy to have him there. Shit, the security of having a man around felt good, too.

A month went by, and no phone calls from Walter. I was finally relaxed and was ready to go out and get my shit together again. Aries called and wanted to meet with me. "It's not safe yet," I told her, "but I'll meet with you soon. It's for your own sake—Walter won't have mercy on anybody who's dealt with me. We can talk via cell phone, but no face-to-face until I feel it's a little more secure for us."

Everybody was so upset at Walter, but he didn't care. He felt that everybody helped me and that nobody cared about him or his feelings. That wasn't it. In my heart I knew that something was going on in Walter's head, but I couldn't help to save him. I even started to miss him a little bit. I decided to call him. He answered quickly and began crying.

"Stop crying, Walter," I said. "Do you want to see your son?" I agreed to meet him at his grandmother's home. I came an hour earlier than the time we agreed to meet, and he was so happy to see Junior and me. I told Walter that I would be back in a couple of hours to pick up Junior. This was my opportunity to go see Harmony, my mom, and Aries. So I did.

I spent an hour with Harmony and my mom. They wanted to know where I was living and I refused to tell. "I'm okay," I said. "Once I get into a better environment, I'll let you know ASAP." They gave me a hug and a kiss and some money and told me to take care of the baby and myself. "Okay, I'll be in touch soon," I promised. I said my good-byes and left. I called Aries and told her I was on my way to her house. To my surprise, she had moved out of her parents' house. I was so happy for her. I pulled up at Mrs. Carmichael's home. Aries ran out so fast and grabbed me and wouldn't let me go. I was happy to see her, too. I had missed her a lot. We talked about everything but where I was living. I refused to let her know where I was living; I was not too happy to tell my living arrangements.

"As soon as I get a better place," I said, "you're invited to come and stay." I hugged her, and we cried and cried, and then I left. I had to get my baby from his dad.

As I again pulled up to Walter's grandmother's house, I noticed that there was police all over the neighborhood. I panicked—police were walking out of Sweetie's house with Big Cousin—he was in handcuffs. I soon learned that he'd beat up Walter.

At last, somebody was on my side. I wished I'd been there to see it. I really don't believe in violence, but that was one ass-whipping I would have loved to have seen. I grabbed my baby and left.

The long drive back to the hotel made me so tired. Pooky came down and got Junior, gave him a bath, and put him to sleep for me. I thanked him and went to bed. I'd had a long day and needed to sleep.

I checked my phone when I woke up the next day—I had missed six phone calls and had three messages. The numbers were all blocked so I couldn't call back. My messages were from Omar. He was in town and hoped that he could hook up with me.

Of course I agreed, even though I couldn't call him back to respond. I waited and waited and finally he called me.

I was so excited to see him. I had no bruises or scratches on my body, but I knew that I would have to tell Omar everything; I really did want him to know. I always felt like there was something between us and maybe now was a good time to find out. We arranged to meet in a crowded place downtown for dinner and a movie. I had just enough time to get an outfit and call Aries. "I'm coming right over," she insisted. "I'll help you get ready for your date with Omar." I agreed, and she made me even more beautiful for the evening. After I got dressed, Aries did my makeup and thank God I did hair. I was so fly. I knew that once Omar saw me, he would be thrilled to be with me tonight. I smiled as Aries took my picture, and then I left.

Once at the restaurant, I walked in with confidence. I knew I looked good—all eyes were on me. I got some of my confidence back; nothing could go wrong that night. I wore a dress that was so sexy that I could have posed for *Elle* magazine.

Omar called my name in his soft-spoken voice. I paused for a second before I turned around. Tears of joy ran down my face; I was so happy to see him. I felt we never had time to really get to know each because I was stuck on stupid.

Well, there was a new sheriff in town, and I was looking to make things right. Omar looked so good. He reminded me of the actor Taye Diggs. So sexy, so muscular, and a big—oh, hell, you know. I couldn't stop staring at him. He made me feel so good being next to him.

"So, what's new with you, Tracee?"

"I'm not with Walter, if that's what you're asking."

"I was going to ask you that next. Do you want to talk about it?" he asked.

"Sure, why not? I don't know where to start."

"Start wherever it is comfortable for you, baby," he suggested.

"Omar, let me tell you about me," I began. "I thought Walter was the one for me, but he was not. I would like to know what you expect from me, and then I can tell you everything."

Omar smiled. "Well, first of all, I've missed you, and I think about you so much. I tried to move on, but I couldn't. I came back to see if we could try again."

I reached over to touch his hand. "Omar, I left Walter. He beat me so much, to the point that I forgot what we were fighting about and why we were fighting. I got tired of it, and I left with my baby. I refuse to go back. I was sick of him treating me like shit. He had total control of my life. I was in love, and I loved him so.

"At one point I felt that he beat me because he loved me, and I wasn't going to leave him. I got so used to it that it became an every-other-day beating. I knew how to cover up so well that I was amazed. One day, I got tired and went to have lunch with Aries instead of going to work, and he I guess followed me to the restaurant. When I woke up, I realized that he had knocked me out.

"Enough was enough. I'm looking for a new place right now. I have my cousin Pooky staying with me for protection. I know Walter will not try anything with him around. I need to be secure, so we have an arrangement until I get back fully on my feet."

"Oh, baby, I'm so sorry to hear this," Omar said. "Why did you not call me?"

"Omar, I had to get out of this relationship, and I didn't want you getting involved in it."

"Too late now because I'm very much so getting involved. Tracee, I knew the day I met you years ago that you could feel me. I know now I feel you even more. Let's try to have a great dinner. Later, we can talk about us in a quieter place."

We ordered our meals and just laughed and talked for about two hours. I excused myself to make a phone call to check on my son.

Pooky answered. "Junior is fine," he told me. "Have a good time—you deserve it."

I did just that. Omar and I caught up on a lot of things in both of our lives. We walked through the courtyards of the mall area where we had dinner. It was lovely. I had a great time. Omar asked me to stay, but I told him that this wasn't a good time. "Maybe when you come back into town we can get together again," I suggested.

He agreed and gave me such a good night kiss that I knew I would never forget it.

"I'll keep in touch," I promised, "and maybe come out to see you if you want me to."

Omar asked me to call him when I got home so we could talk ourselves to sleep. When I got home I told Pooky about my date with Omar. Pooky was so happy for me. He told me that he and Aries had fun tonight, too. OMFG! I could only imagine.

I took a long, hot shower because temptation was eating me alive at that point. I wanted to go with Omar, but I knew I couldn't go with him. In the shower, I cried until I couldn't cry anymore. I needed Omar to make me feel like a woman again. He cared about me; I knew it. I always felt like he did anyway. The first time we met, I felt a true connection with him. Now, I felt that same connection all over again. Omar taught me how to set an e-mail address account so we could shoot e-mails from time to time.

Weeks turned into months. I missed my friend but I was finally getting back into the swing of things. I went back to work full time and asked Pooky to become my babysitter for Junior. Pooky was happy to do so—he was becoming a changed man after being with me for so long. I liked his being around me, and it was good for Junior to have a father figure.

One Monday morning my phone started ringing off the hook. Every time I answered it, someone would hang up. Finally,

I got mad and yelled at the person on the other line, but there was no response. Two hours later, Omar called and insisted that I check my e-mail. I told him today was different and I was out taking care of business.

I found a new place to live—a condo—and reacted quickly so we could get into it right away. I had enough money to pay rent for six months. I signed my new lease and went back to the front leasing office to check my e-mail that Omar had sent.

To my surprise, he let me know that he was picked up by a major league team. He also wanted to see me immediately. I responded to him and told him that I was moving and that I didn't have any more money because I'd paid my lease up for six months. Also, I told him that I didn't have furniture to put in my apartment. He called me on my phone and told me exactly this: "I'm coming there in two days for a week, and we will take care of everything." I said, "Who is we and take care of what?"

He said, "Your apartment. No woman of mine will be without furniture, so I'm coming with my agent to do business, and I will help you furnish your new place. Tracee, I want you to go out and find everything you want, so I can write you a check to cover your expenses."

I was so happy. I hadn't even slept with Omar, but he was helping out already.

Omar was man of his word. He wrote me a check for seven thousand dollars. I took that right to the bank and bought everything I needed for my condo. It wasn't fully furnished, but I was thankful for his graciousness.

I invited him over for an intimate dinner for two. He was excited to see how I had furnished my condo. He seemed surprised that it wasn't done. "Baby, why didn't you tell me that it wasn't enough money to complete your new home?"

"Omar, I was happy to get that money from you! Do you think that I could or would complain? I can get the rest of the furnishings later. Thank you so much for doing this for me."

"Well, before I leave I'm going to give you some more money to finish so that when I come back I want can see the finished results."

After going back and forth, I agreed with Omar and asked him to spend his last night here with me. He didn't reject my offer. We cuddled, and I cried tears of joy while he lay next to me. The whole night, we didn't even have sex. He didn't try, so I didn't either. The next morning, a limo picked him up. He gave me a kiss and left. Later, I called to thank him again—I'd found a check for twenty thousand dollars on my dresser—and I asked him to send for me once he got settled.

A month went by; then Omar set up a date to fly me to Miami. He told me that all I needed was my purse; he would take care of the rest. I made arrangements at work and with Pooky to watch Junior while I would be out of town.

Nearly two weeks later, as my trip was approaching, I called Omar but there was no answer. I didn't like how our phone communication was anyway. The day before I was to leave, he called me back to make sure I was heading to the airport. I was, and but I was upset at the same time. I made sure I was very sexy as I flew into Miami.

After a long flight, I got off the plane and found there was a man standing at the gate, holding a sign with my name on it. Omar had hired a driver to pick me up. I was laughing and as soon as I got to the limo, Omar jumped out and kissed me with such passion.

"I missed you so much! I'm so sorry for being rude and not calling you back! I just wanted to be surprised when you got here. Instead, I'm even happier than ever." Who could be mad at a man who went all out to impress me? "What would you like to do first?" he asked. Now, in the back of mind I really wanted him to tear my dress off and make hot love in the back of the limo, but I said, "Can we get some attire for me to wear while I'm here? You told me to fly without clothes, so I did."

"Okay, baby," he agreed. "Let's go do some shopping." He told the limo driver where to take me and off we drove. As we pulled up to a huge mall, I saw Hummers, Bentleys, and BMWs all parked outside the mall. I thought, *What kind of mall is this?*

The driver opened the door and we got out. I was dressed so sexy that Omar just couldn't stop staring at my ass. I whispered in his ear, "Do you like what you see?" He licked his lips and responded, "*Yes!*"

He took me to five different stores. I must have spent two thousand to three thousand dollars in each store on clothes and shoes. I felt like I was taking advantage of Omar and suggested that we leave the mall.

"Are you okay?" he asked.

"Omar, I don't feel comfortable spending your money like this—this is not what I'm about."

I must have upset him because he was quiet the whole ride back to his house. We drove for forty-five minutes to an hour and finally pulled up to a gated community. There were maybe a total of ten houses on the property. I was amazed at how beautiful the houses were. They were huge—at least ten to fifteen thousand square feet per home.

There was one house that was so big, I was in total awe of it. To my surprise, it was Omar's house.

"Damn, baby," I said, "you're doing big now." I got out, and the driver took my bags and brought them to the front door. That damn door was at least fifteen feet tall. I couldn't wait to see the inside of this remarkable home. I knew it was going to be gorgeous on the inside.

Omar grabbed my hand and pressed his body against mine from behind. "Let's go see our new home, okay, baby?"

I was weak in the knees—all of this in one day was a lot to deal with for gal like me. I walked in, expecting to see fabulous furnishings ... and it was fucking empty. I couldn't believe it. It was *empty*. I smiled ... and then burst out laughing.

"Baby, this is why I haven't called you back," Omar explained. "I was waiting to get the keys, and I also was worried that the house wasn't going to be ready by the time you got here. So, do you like it or what?"

"I love it. It's ... it's ... so damn big. When are you getting the furniture?"

"I was hoping you could help me decorate while you are here."

"Sure, I would love to help you."

"Great! I'm having an interior designer come by tomorrow, and you came do whatever you want to the house. After all, you will be living here soon."

My mouth was stuck wide open. At first, I couldn't speak a word. I finally managed to say, "Omar, we have to talk."

"Okay, baby, let's go upstairs to the master bedroom and talk."

"Why does the master bedroom have furniture in it? Omar, what is going on?"

"I need you in my life, Tracee. I really do. When I left Vegas this last time, I felt the need to start getting my shit together, and I wanted it to be with you. I want babies, and I want you to have my babies."

"Red flag! Did you forget that I already have a son?"

"Not at all, baby. I need to know if this is where you want to be. Can you move down here to be with me? I can't do this career without a strong woman like you by my side. I promise I'm going to do right by you and show you things that I would never show or do for any women but you, baby. Sleep on it, and take your time. We will talk about it a little later, okay?"

"I need longer than a day, Omar. This is a lot to process overnight."

"I bought you something while you were enjoying your day shopping. I had a sales associate get you some nightgowns and panties. Which ones do you prefer to wear?"

How about nothing at all? I went from 0 to 60 seconds of undressing him, and we made passionate love all night long—and I do mean all night long. He made me tingle, and he told me I made his toes curl. I was so tired that I had no energy to get up and deal the designer the next morning. I rolled over, and Omar was right there. He looked at me and said, "Please don't disappoint me, Tracee. Please don't do it." After that night of lovemaking, I just couldn't believe he had enough energy to go another round with me. *He did!*

It was so good—so, so good. I was very impressed with his skills. I got up and showered, and he joined me, of course, and it was on again. I brushed my teeth and pulled my hair into a ponytail; then went downstairs to meet the designer.

It was a French married couple who owned the interior design company called Le Designs. They we really nice and offered to teach me French in the process of putting some color schemes and patterns together. Omar refused to get involved; he made it clear that this was all on me. Six long hours and nine books later, we finally put together a showroom house. They were so eager to get started, but Omar said they had to wait until next week to begin. He wrote a check to them, and that was it. I felt that after making such big decisions on his new home that I could ask him what kind of a contract deal he got.

He looked at me and said, "Do you love me?"

I thought about it and I said, "I do have feelings for you and I love you, but I'm not *in love* yet."

"Well, when you fall in love with me, then I will tell you."

I didn't know what to say after that. We got dressed and went to pick out some furniture for all the other rooms. Before we left, I walked through the whole house and discovered that there were seven bedrooms and nine bathrooms. A six-car garage had vehicles parked in each stall.

As we were walking out to the garage, the house phone rang. It was Omar's mother, Mrs. Gianni Velasquez. She fussed and yelled at him for a good twenty minutes. He told her that she had to meet me and that we were on our way.

We got into his two-door Rolls-Royce and left. This car was so clean, it was white on white—cocaine white, with Omar's initials on the headrest of the seats. His mother lived about thirty minutes from him. I was excited to meet her. Omar mentioned to me that his mother's English wasn't very good and that she probably would speak a little Spanish in the conversation. In my opinion, that's code for "none of your damn business."

I wore my new sexy long-flowing dress to his mother's beautiful home. As soon as we got to the front door, I saw that the house was full of people. It was a family get-together, but Omar didn't seem to happy to be part of it. When I met everyone, though, they made me feel welcome—I knew I had that effect on people.

Shortly after we arrived, the doorbell rang—and that's when the drama started. A pregnant woman wobbled through the front door and started to cuss out Omar. She pointed at me and yelled, "You better tell her who I am, or I will do it for you!" My stomach dropped. All I could think about was how Omar had lied to me and that this lady was his women.

"Tracee, this is my stupid-ass sister Jessica. She is pregnant by one of my teammates, and I get all the shit because he won't deal with her."

"Hi, hello, and nice to meet you sweetie. Are you here to stay or are you just visiting?"

I replied, "Both!"

"Well, well, well, I see Omar found a woman with some guts. Come here, girl. You are all right with me."

At first I thought I was going to have to beat a bitch down at Omar's momma's house. After all, I was the new girl on the scene.

"So, momma, how long are you going to be here?"

"I'm leaving on Monday, so about a week."

"Well, we will have to do lunch, if you can get away from my brother."

"Sure, if he doesn't mind, I would love it."

Everybody was really down-to-earth, and Omar's momma kept smiling at me and saying that she hoped I would keep Omar grounded because he hadn't had much luck with women. *So that was the problem that Omar was having—no good luck. I'll have to remember to talk to him about that tonight when we get back home.* We ended up staying out at his mother's home for four hours, and he was pissed.

"Baby, let's go because we have so much to do!"

"All right, let me tell everybody bye, and we can leave." I gave his sister my number so we could talk. I felt like I could get all the info I needed on Omar from her.

Omar and I left and then made our first stop at the furniture depot. This store had great bedroom sets, and Omar ended up buying three sets. We set up delivery for two weeks later to give the designers the time to paint and add art décor on the walls.

By this time Omar was ready to eat. "You're eating a lot," I told him. And he replied, "I'm just happy to see you. I eat when I'm happy." He wanted Mexican food so we went to a bar and grill on South Beach. The food was so good.

I didn't want to put a damper in our day, but I had to ask a question: "Omar, if for some reason things don't go the way you expect them to, are you okay with dealing with things by yourself?"

He paused, gave me a smile, and said, "T, there is things that I want, and there are people I need in my life. As far as taking care of business without you, I can, but do I want to? No. After all, Tracee, you act like you don't want to be here."

"Did I say that?"

"Your actions are showing how ungrateful you're becoming. I don't want to start an argument with you, Tracee, but if you want to get it poppin', shit, we can."

"I'm actually trying, Omar, but you put me in a situation that I wasn't prepared for. I thought I was coming to hang out with you, and all you're trying to do is give me wifely duties. I want to enjoy seeing you. It's been a while. I miss you. I also don't mind helping you with your home, but do you really want me here?" I looked at him and saw that he was getting pissed at me.

The drive home was intense—he didn't even say a thing to me—so I had to break the ice. I leaned over to kiss him on the cheek, but he pushed my face.

I was stunned! *No, this nigga didn't.* I was trying to have our day out continue to be a good day, not a bad day. I was mad, but not mad. I had started the fight, so I was trying to make it right. He wouldn't let me fix it.

I decided to really act like an asshole. "So now 'cause you can't have your way, your going to pout like a little baby, huh, Omar? Maybe you need a little reality check from me, Omar. It's not about what you want. I want a lot of things, too, but I'm not pouting to get what I want. I can't believe you're upset. You need to grow up!"

"Tracee, we are going home. I need to cool off. I'm frustrated, confused, and disappointed with you. I really, really am."

"Whatever, Omar."

The rest of the ride home was very quiet. I wanted to laugh. I knew I had to keep a serious face, but it was funny to me. I had to make him believe that he was in charge, so I was silent until we pulled up in the driveway. I knew that I could make it right once we got in the house. Omar jumped into the shower, and I lay on the bed. His phone starting ringing like crazy. He yelled, "Baby, can you answer it?"

"Hello," I said to the caller. To my surprise, it was a woman. She replied, "Can I talk to Omar?"

"He's in the shower. Can I take a message?"

"This is Summer!"

I paused; then I replied, "Okay, and what is this regarding?"

Then the woman hung up! I went right into the shower and threw Omar's phone at him. Then I yelled, "Who is Summer, and why did she hang up on me?"

He started laughing and then told me to put on something nice because we had an appearance to make tonight at a local hot-spot club.

I got dressed and got a little too sexy for my damn self. I knew exactly what to do to get Omar's undivided attention through the night. I put on my "I know he is going to watch me and so is everybody else" dress and walked out to the garage. He was waiting so patiently. As the Rolls started down the road, I asked Omar again, "Who is Summer?"

"Summer ain't nobody, so leave it alone."

I sat with an attitude the whole way there. We pulled up to the club—and the night went down hill from there. The cameras were flashing and the media was everywhere. There wasn't any place to turn to get away from it. I gave them the true diva—I thought it was about me for one hot second. I was definitely going to get my thirty seconds of fame. We finally got through the crowd to the VIP section of the club. There were all kinds of ballers in the area of the club. Everywhere I turned my head, there was a man and a fine one. We sat down, and then some of Omar's teammates came up to us. They wanted to know who I was.

Omar introduced me as his woman, although we hadn't really established what I was to him. I leaned over to whisper in his ear. "Oh, now I'm your girl." He had one heck of a smile on his face—it was from the attention he was receiving from his teammates.

After all, I was real sexy. Shit, if I wasn't so damn cute, I would give myself my own damn phone number. It's a real thang to say right here, right now! I loved all the attention, but Omar loved it more than I did. We drank so much in the club that I was too intoxicated to remember where we were. Omar realized it was getting late; he grabbed my hand—at least, I thought he did—and pulled me toward the door. All of a sudden, I felt a tug on my dress. It was Omar—I was holding another man's hand.

Omar grabbed me and yelled at me. "Get yo' stupid ass in the car! I go to the bathroom, and your ass is walking out with another dude. You are so trifling, Tracee. When we get home, pack yo' shit."

I fell fast asleep in the car on the way home. It didn't click in my head until we pulled into the driveway. He yelled at me and told me to get out of his car. I couldn't move, and I couldn't focus. Omar ran to the passenger side of the Rolls-Royce and snatched me right out of the damn front seat. He pulled me into the house and yelled at me. I passed out! When I woke up the next morning, he had all of my shit packed. I was still in last night's outfit. I went to talk to him.

"What's going on, Omar? Why do you have all of my clothes packed?"

He replied, "Don't act like you don't know what you did last night."

"What did I do? I don't remember a damn thing."

"Tracee, I went to use the bathroom, and when I came back, you were holding hands with another guy. To add insult to injury, you were leaving with him."

"I don't recall anything, Omar. I really don't remember."

CHAPTER 4

Loving My Life

A FTER THE LONG DEBATE ABOUT WHAT I DID REMEMBER, I apologized to Omar. I really couldn't recall any of my actions of last night. Omar was mad. He did accept my apology, but I knew that it wasn't over.

I took a shower and when I got out, he was gone. I called his cell phone, but he didn't answer. I called his phone for three and half hours. He was truly mad at me—he did pack my shit and tell me to leave his home.

I started crying because I didn't have a clue how to fix this problem. I wanted Omar badly, but I wanted to make things right between us. I felt like he needed to let off steam. The tension was fucked up between us. I waited and waited, but no Omar.

The sun was going down, but he still hadn't answered or returned my phone calls. I had all day to think about what I had done. Once he came back, I would take care of everything. I tried one more time to contact him; this time he answered. I begged him to forgive me.

In his soft-spoken voice, he said he needed some time to cool off. He'd gone to hit some balls on the field, and cell phones weren't allowed on the field. At that point I didn't care where he was; I just wanted him home so I could make things right between us.

"Omar, I need to talk to you. I need you to come home." He replied, "I'm pulling up into the garage right now." The door opened, and I ran to him and kissed him. He did not push my face this time. "I couldn't remember what I did," I explained. "I am so sorry for whatever I did."

He forgave me! We had sex, sex, and mo' sex! Did I forget to mention *sex?* I looked at him, and the passion in his eyes was breathtaking. We both needed to release some of the frustration from last night. Oh, boy, did we do just that!

I knew what I loved about my Omar. When it came time to kiss and make up, we did. We were back happy again and as usual the drama would eventually start up again. About midnight, Omar's phone started vibrating. As any woman would do, I picked it up.

It was Summer! She had left a voice message. I listened to it over and over again. I was very angry. Omar had lied to me about who she was and where he was. The next reaction was not a good reaction from me. I jumped on top of him and slapped him. He grabbed me and threw me to the ground. "What is your problem, Tracee?"

"You lied to me about where and who you were with. The field? For real, Omar? How about Summer?"

"What are you talking about? I haven't been with her."

"Well, according to your voice mail that she left, you guys were together all day today. I guess you really were hitting something. All I can say is wow … *wow!* I didn't unpack my clothes from earlier today, so I'm ready to go now!"

"There are no flights right this minute."

"Well, I will wait and call in the early morning so I can get the hell out of here. You threw a fit about me and all this time, you were the one cheating! You had to have your cake and eat it too! You are so selfish and evil. You only care about your feelings and not anyone else. I'm so glad I didn't move or fully commit to you or this relationship. You have not changed. There is one thing for sure: you got some good dick, but I can get that any time and from anyone."

"Tracee, just because Summer called me it doesn't mean I was with her. Do you really want to know who she is? Fine; I will tell you who she is. I did mess with her, but she will not let go. She is pregnant, and she keeps telling me that it's my baby. I wasn't with her and yes, the condom did break. The dates don't add up. She is harassing me for money, and until the baby is born I will not support her at all."

"Omar, is it yours?"

"Tracee, as far as I know, no. When this whole situation started, I told her you were coming—she knew about you. She told me she would do everything in her power to keep me from being happy. She found out where I lived and followed me to the facility. I saw her when I came out; she wouldn't leave. I offered to talk with her because you and I were fighting. I know that this isn't what you wanted to hear, but oh, well. Also, she said that she would keep coming to my house until I met up with her. I felt that today was that day. I really love you, and I would do anything to keep us together. Tracee, it is all about you and me. I don't need the drama; I don't want the drama. I want a real relationship with you. I have all these strong feelings for you, but I don't want to push you into something you really don't want to be involved in. I brought you here to spend some time with me and to see what can be yours. If you're not ready, then say that. You don't have to lead me on. All I ask is that you is up front with me."

"Omar, you hid the fact that Summer could possibly be carrying your baby. This whole situation is making me sick. I don't know what else to say."

"Baby, I need you in my life—just remember that. Tracee, you have me under a spell that I can't cure. The baby is due in three weeks; at least, that is what she is telling me. I want you to stay at least until then. By the time the baby is born, I hope that you will have made a decision about where you wanna be. I don't mean to hurt you. I never meant to hurt you, if I did. I know I'm insecure about something, but about loving you I am not. Tracee, you're so special, and now that you're going through your mess with your ex, I just want to be supportive of you."

"Omar, I want you so bad, but I'm so scared. You want me to move here. but I don't know anyone. You want me to give up my career back at home. You want me to leave everything that I worked so hard to get. What do I gain, Omar?"

"What? First of all, you gain a *man*, a secure and stable environment for your son, a home you can call *ours*, a new family to call *yours*, and most importantly, *me*! I can show you better than I can tell you. I just need the opportunity. I thought maybe if you met my family that maybe your feelings to stay would change. I don't have anybody that I trust other than you. You are fully aware of the women that I have dated, and you also are aware of each situation, except for this bullshit with Summer. The only reason I didn't tell you about it was because I was so sure that it wasn't mine. I don't need the press involved in my life with the negativity about whether or not the baby is, in fact, mine. Summer slept with a least two or three of my teammates, and I was sick when I found out. We all have to take a paternity test as soon as possible. I need you to stay, to be right here by my side."

"So, let me get this straight: you want me to be here to find out if this hood-rat's baby is yours? Wow, this is some 'Days of Our Stupid Decision Lives,' and I'm a costar in your drama series. You co-wrote and produced this wild shit. I do have a conscience and yes, I do want to find out if this is your baby. I need to contact Pooky and send for my son."

"Thank you so much, Tracee. I will call my travel agent to fly them out immediately."

"I have to talk to Pooky first. Give me another day to decide if I can stay another three weeks. I need to call Pooky right now. May I use your house phone please?" I quickly dialed, and Pooky picked up on the third ring. "Pooky, this Tracee, and I need to speak with you about some things. How is Junior?"

"He misses you! Tracee, girl, don't tell me you beat up this man."

"Naw, fool, but I did slap him silly."

"What's going down in Miami?"

"Omar needs me to stay a little longer, and I was wondering if you wanted to fly down with Junior."

"Miami? Hell, yeah! How long are we staying?"

"I need three more weeks here. If you want, you can stay that long as well."

"T, all I need is a week, and I'll come back to Vegas to chill until you come home."

"That sounds great, so let me make the flight arrangements, and I'll call you back in an hour or so."

"I'll start packing, but do you need me to bring some clothes to you?"

"No, Omar took me shopping. If I run out of clothes within the next couple of weeks, I will go buy whatever I need. Hey, so start getting your stuff together, and I will call you back with your flight details." I hung up with Pooky and went to talk with Omar.

"Baby, what did Pooky say?"

"He said yes!"

"Cool beans. Let me call my travel agent and set up their flights." Omar walked upstairs and handled his business.

The doorbell rang—it was the designers. I couldn't figure out why they were back because I had made our next appointment perfectly clear. "Hey, what are you guys doing here so early today?"

"Omar called and said we needed to get this house going because you were arranging for your family to come and stay."

"He did? Well, get your butts in here, and let's get right to it!"

"We have some furniture companies that are willing to help get you fully furnished with a week. Can you handle that?"

"Absolutely!"

"Let's go to the showroom floor because they have everything in a big warehouse."

"I need to get dressed and so does Omar. Give me twenty minutes to get ready." I ran upstairs to tell Omar to get ready to go. He was busy with the travel agent, so he suggested that I follow the designers to the store. He gave me the keys to his Range Rover. I put on a long, flowing summer dress, grabbed my purse, and headed down the stairs.

All of a sudden, Omar yelled, "Tracee, here is my credit card to use." I looked at him, but before I could say a thing, he said, "Don't worry; the company is fully aware of you coming in to use my card."

"How?"

"I bought furniture before from them when I had my small condo, and I told them my future wife would, hopefully, help me finish my new home."

"You are not slick, Omar; you're not! It amazes me how just an hour ago, I was leaving your ass for good, and now I'm going to go buy some furniture. I must really love you, Omar. I really must."

He gave me a kiss, and we were off to do some major damage on the credit card. I followed the designers to a store called Mostic Cole Juarez Contemporary Designs. This store was huge. I already knew this was not going to be easy. I left my cell phone at the house, so I couldn't call Omar at all. We went through the entire store, picking out bedroom sets for each room, and a living room set, and a formal dining room set. This store had everything from rugs, to lamps, to mirrors, to wall art. I was able to furnish the entire house.

After three long hours of shopping, Omar pulled up to the furniture store. "So, how are you doing with all of this?"

"I'm just about done. I'm waiting to see how long before they can deliver all of the furniture to your house."

"*Our* house, Tracee. *Our* house."

"The designers helped me from top to bottom. In fact, you will have the most laid-out house on the block."

"Dang, you did all this in a matter of three hours."

"Yep! I now know why you didn't want to do it, Omar."

"So, Tracee, what is the grand total?"

"I am waiting to find that out!"

The sales manager walked up to Omar and said, "Omar, your home will be beautifully decorated. I would like to personally thank you for shopping with us. If there is anything else you need, feel free to let us know. We are taking 30 percent off of your grand total for today also. Your total is $85,675.39."

My mouth dropped to the floor. "Omar, I did not mean to spend so much money."

"Tracee, it's fine. I thought you were going to spend more than that, but you did real good. I can't believe you furnished the entire house for that little bit of money. That's not bad for the entire house. Sir, when do you expect to deliver all of this?"

"Omar, we can start as early as tomorrow. It will be an all-day event. I need a window of six hours. I will have three trucks and a crew of nine men to set up your entire home."

"Thanks! Tracee will be there to let you guys in."

"Also, Omar, we will call thirty-five minutes before we come to assure that someone will be home. Thank you again, and have a great day."

Omar was so excited—at least, that was the impression I got from the look on his face. I knew we were starting to progress with each other. I was happy, too. I got back into the truck and drove back to the mansion.

Omar followed me. "Hey, do you want to go get a quick bite to eat?"

"Sure, where are you taking me today?"

"This soul-food restaurant called Beaudreaux's Bayou, in South Beach. I heard it was so good, so I want to try it."

"Omar, do you know what the dress code is?"

"Casual, I think. You have plenty of those flowing dresses, so put on one of those."

"I sure will. Thanks for the suggestion." I put on a little Mac lip gloss and some Vera Wang perfume and walked to the truck. I was so hungry. All that furniture shopping made me feel weak and tired at the same time. I was eager to get to this joint. I expected it to be good. It took us twenty-five minutes to get there. When we arrived, the entire restaurant was fully aware of who Omar was.

The owner and his chef of VIP services met us. I have to admit that I liked all of the perks of being with a celebrity. Omar was top-notch. The entire state knew he was making over twenty million dollars a season. It had been blasted all over the news.

I hated that part, but liked everything else. There were many circumstances to dating, marrying, and having children with these types of athletes. I heard of all the bullshit because women would tell me the horrible stories back home. I was now going to experience living with a wealthy, high-profile man. There was nothing to stop me from doing it. Omar arranged for Pooky and Junior to arrive in Miami tomorrow morning. I was so excited, I couldn't sit still—I missed both of them.

Omar and I sat at the bar and had a couple of drinks. Mr. Howard, the owner of the restaurant, was setting up our VIP table so we would not be disturbed. It was so laid-out. The lights from the city of Miami were so breathtaking, and the décor of the restaurant was colorful. I thought I was in a nightclub instead of a restaurant.

A live band played jazz music, setting the mood just right. I had my man on the side of me and my family on the way to be with me. I had it all in the palm of my hands. A staff member came to our table to greet us.

Omar's phone kept ringing so much as we got our eat on. I was actually getting upset with him and that damn phone. I couldn't figure out who was calling so much.

I was tempted to throw that phone clear across the room, but I didn't want to become "boo-ghetto." I was trying to be ladylike and a tad ghetto at the same time. I mean, I was out of my environment. I needed to adapt. I needed something to drink—something heavy to drink. When the waiter came to our table, I ordered a Remy on the rocks. "Matter of fact, make it a double."

Omar paused for a second and then laughed. "I'll have the same." He whispered in my ear, which he knew turned me on, saying, "I have a little surprise for you tonight."

What could it be? Omar could truly pull off anything that he wanted to. The band was gigging. I was enjoying it so much that Omar asked me to dance. As we strolled over to the dance floor, I heard a voice over the microphone. It was Knight McBrian! As I stood there, my legs went numb. My hands were sweaty. I couldn't breath. I had to pee. I had the bubble guts—all this shit at the same time.

Omar grabbed my hand and got down on his knee. He asked me to stay with him, to be with him, to *marry* him! *Oh, Lord! Help me!*

This whole restaurant shit was a setup. He'd had every intention of doing this. I should have known that Omar was up to no good. He had me helping him decorate to get me in a good mood for tonight. There was no way in hell I was leaving on a plane. He had a plan from the get-go. He told me that he would never let me go, once he got me back in his arms. I fell for it, too. It was romantic to have a celebrity sing to get me in the mood.

Knight was singing my favorite song, "Anytime." Omar said this was the song that he listened to every day when we were apart. "Baby, I hope you like what I have done," he whispered in my ear, "'cause it only gets better."

"Better than Knight? I can't wait to see this."

Knight kissed my hand and handed Omar the microphone.

"Ladies and gentlemen, I'm pleased to announce that you all are here to meet and help celebrate my wife-to-be, Tracee— if she excepts my proposal." *What proposal?* "Tracee, will you marry me?"

I gladly accepted by yelling, "*Yes!*" As we sat back down, strangers approached us to congratulate us on our new life together. I reached for my drink—and there was a little box right next to it. Inside the box was a very large diamond ring.

I had a lot to tell Omar, but I wanted to wait until we drove back to the mansion. Then I said, "Omar, we need to talk."

"First, let me get everything off of my chest. Tracee, can we make love? I put on one heck of a show tonight to convince you how much I love you."

"Baby, don't you think everything is moving too fast?"

"Tracee, there is nothing I would rather do, right here, right now, than marry you. I need you, and I want you to myself. I can't let you get away this time. I promised myself that I would never let you go again. It's you and me now, and that's how I like it, Tracee."

"Did you forget about the girl and that baby?"

"I told you, that's not my baby. We will find out soon." Omar checked his phone; Summer called and had left a message.

"What's the message" I asked.

"She had the baby and wants to know if we could come up to the hospital right away. Hell, nah! Not tonight. We just got engaged, and nobody is going to ruin this night. How about we go tomorrow?"

I agreed. Let's get home for some engagement sex. Okay! I don't have to explain how the night went. I swear he was trying to make a baby. Thank you for birth control. We don't need any new drama added just yet.

Omar called Summer early in the afternoon to let her know we were coming. Omar, yes, baby, after this whole baby-mamma drama is done, can you change your phone number please! Anything for you, baby. Anything!

We dressed and drove to the hospital. I was wearing my new ring, and I wanted to go shopping for Omar's after we left the hospital. I stopped to grab some balloons, candy, and a teddy bear for new baby.

"Omar, what did she have?"

"A boy!"

"Cool." I grabbed my items and left the gift shop. When we got to her room, the baby was asleep. I took the first look and saw that the baby had nice hair. I needed to look and examine the baby for Omar's features. First of all, Omar was chocolate-skinned like Taye Diggs and had lips like LL Cool J. I didn't see any of those distinctive appearances on the baby. "What is his name?" I asked.

"Ortiz."

"Full name, please!"

"Ortiz Omar Gonyalo."

I'd hoped that she hadn't given the baby Omar's name. I was a little upset that his name was included.

"Wow, so are those the names of the potential baby daddies?"

"*No!*" she yelled.

I did what any women would do; I stared the baby down. He didn't have dark spots on his ears or his hands. Omar has nice hands and feet. The baby did, too. He was cute, but he didn't favor Omar at all.

"So, when do I schedule a blood test, Summer?"

"I'm going to ask the doctor when she comes back in to check the baby."

"How long?"

"There is the doctor, so ask her now."

"Excuse me, I need to schedule a paternity test for this baby."

"Are you a potential father?" the doctor asked.

I answered for him. "We are not sure, ma'am, so we would like to have the test done at his doctor's office. It is more convenient for us to have it done there, for privacy reasons."

"Not a problem, sir. Just have your doctor call my office, and we will set up everything. Here is my card, and if you have any questions, just call."

"Thanks." I grabbed her card and read "Dr. Angela Marilyn, Pediatrics Specialist."

We both stared at the baby, and then we said our good-byes. As we walked through the hospital, Omar got sad.

"What's your problem?" I asked.

He looked at me and said, "Baby, I know I'm not the father, but what if she can't find his daddy?"

"Omar, this not our problem. We need to wait for the results and then move forward."

"All right. Tracee, can you call to set up the test for a day this week?"

Later, I called his doctor's office and explained what we needed to have done.

They took care of everything. They said that once they set a time for Summer and the baby to come in, they then would set a time for us. Cool beans.

"Let's go and do something fun, Omar. Like what, you ask? Let's go to the beach."

"That's cool; I like the beach. South Beach okay, baby?"

I bought a cute, itty-bitty bikini on the way to the beach and changed right into it. I bought some sunscreen and water. We laid out for about an hour. I got sunburned so quickly that I was ready to go. Some females approached Omar while I was lying beside him. They were flirting their asses off. I had to put the check down. "Ah, excuse me, but he is in a relationship now, so roll out." All Omar could do was laugh. I had to remind him of the way he'd acted that night in the club, and then he didn't think it was so funny.

"Babe, let's try to have a good time. I want this day to go smooth. I got a lot going on, so I want to try to relax. Let's do something we will never forget. Hey, let's get some matching tattoos that symbolize how we feel about each other. I know a great tattoo parlor in the hood. They will hook us up! Let's go home and change. I'll call them so we can get in ASAP."

When we arrived back home, Pooky and Junior were waiting for us in the driveway. I jumped out so fast! I was crying and laughing at the same time.

"I heard you got engaged."

"Who told you that, Pooky?"

"Tracee, why do you think Omar was trying to get us here so fast? When he called me, he told me everything that he was going to do. I hate that I missed it. I hope you said yes. As far as the condo back in Vegas, Omar paid the lease up for a year. I told him I would stay in it. So know you don't have to stress about the condo anymore."

"Wow, so now you and Omar are working together behind my back."

"Shut up, Tracee, it ain't like that at all. Just try to enjoy your new life with him. God only knows how much you need this."

I kissed my baby for so long that his cheeks were red. He was so happy to see his mommy—that's all he yelled. I was trying to get a good look at him, but once he saw the pool, it was a done deal.

"Do you want to go swimming, little man?" Omar asked Junior twice, and he was taking his clothes off. I showed Pooky the house. He was loving it to the fullest.

"Damn, girl, you got a winner. Please do right by him. He must not find out about your past."

"I will never tell a soul, Pooky. You are the only one who knows everything. I didn't even tell Aries."

"Your secret is safe with me. Now, show me the rest of this hotel that you call a mansion."

We grabbed a cocktail as we strolled through the house.

"Tracee, this house is laid out. Who decorated this house?"

"I did," I said, with a smirk on my face.

"I know you did. Omar told me while you were gone with interior designers when I called to check on you."

Wow! He never told me you called. No biggie. Yes, it is, Pooky. Yes, it is. I need to be aware because I don't like sneakiness or foolishness. Girl, this man has asked for your hand in marriage, so don't trip. You need to call your girls and have a big celebration.

I'm listening, so I'll talk with Omar, and we will have to have a big party right before the season starts. Well, where should you have it—in Vegas or Miami? Hum! I'll let you know once I talk to Omar.

So, let's pick out your room that you're going to sleep in. I'll let Junior sleep with us until he gets used to the house. Damn, Tracee, I love this house. Girl, you hit the jackpot.

Later, we sat at the dinner table to discuss when and where to have our big party for both of our families to meet. I wanted to do it Miami and, of course, Omar wanted to do it in Vegas. We needed someone to help us decide, so we asked Omar.

"I got it; let's have it in Las Vegas, Nevada."

"Nevada?"

"What's in Arizona?" Omar asked. "Nothing—that's why we can have one big party where nobody knows anyone. Perfecto!"

"Oh! Omar, please do not start speaking Spanish!"

"Tracee, you're going to have to learn to speak it, so you need to get use to it. Let's talk to our parents and find out if this is going to be a good location for both sides of the families."

I called my girls to tell them the good news. I called Trinity, Cashmere, Aries, Tiny, and Ro-yaltee. They were so excited and, yes, ready to get their party on. I told them that once we set the dates, I would be back in touch with all of them. I called my mom, and she said she would spread the word.

Omar called his friends. I only remembered a few of them, but I knew he had a lot of them. He called Freddy, Jo-Jo, Nahim, Anthony, and, of course, Pedro. These were his Cuban friends that he grew up with. They were happy and ready to go! Then he called his mom, and she couldn't wait to spread the word. Everybody was so happy! I had to admit I was happy, too. It was time to get ready for bed. I had a long day tomorrow, and I needed my rest.

We got Junior ready for bed, and Omar wanted some late nooky. I had to remind him that we had guests in the house, and he checked me real quick. "This house is so big that no one can hear us bang our heads against the headboards anyway." He knew exactly what to say. He knew how to sweet-talk me with just a few words. "Let me hit it from the back! *Hey!*" I turned Jamaican real quick and said, "I t'ink I love he! Yeah, mon!"

Omar and I were meant for each other. I was ready to fully commit to this relationship. I hoped he was, too. We fell fast asleep after we did the nasty. I held him in my arms for the rest of the night.

When we woke up the next morning, the chef had prepared a big breakfast. My new hubby-to-be brought me breakfast in bed. "Wow, baby, thanks!"

"Anything for you, Tracee."

"So is it Vegas or not?"

"Babe, I think it should be here in Miami. I have a lot of family that is illegal, and I can't risk them leaving this state."

"Okay, I will let my momma know what is going on, and she can handle getting in touch with the family members who want to come and celebrate with us."

"All right, and I'll call my mom and let her know that the wedding will be in Miami and the engagement party will be in Vegas. Then it is set. All we need to do is set a date. How about February 14, next year?"

"Omar, is that Valentine's Day?"

"Yep."

"That's six months away!"

"I know."

"This is going to be a special day for the both of us. Omar, I'm so excited."

"I'm very grateful for you, Tracee—for real."

I sat down with a pen and paper to write out all of my ideas of what I wanted. I picked wedding colors and flowers and a theme, of course. I had to get my girls out here to meet his boys to see who we could match up. I grabbed Omar as he walked by and asked if I could invite my girls out for a weekend. "Sure, baby, call up your girls. I'll call up the fellas so we can have some real fun."

It took all that morning to reach all of them. I asked them to fly out the next Friday for the weekend; I would have our travel agent set up flights. I enjoyed the rest of my time with Pooky and Junior. We took them out to the beach and then to the mall to do some shopping. They were having fun! I missed my baby boy so much. I needed him here with me. I knew he needed his mommy, too.

The week went by so fast; soon it was time to take Pooky to the airport. I cried the whole way there. I gave him a hug and a kiss and some money. Pooky thanked me and went into the airport. Junior waved as we drove off. When I pulled back into the driveway, Omar was waiting for us. He smiled and picked up Junior, and we went inside. I showed Omar some wedding colors, and we picked colors that complemented our skin tones.

He picked the flowers and now all we needed was to pick out a cake. I wanted something huge and beautiful. I called a couple of custom bakeries and made appointments for cake-tasting. I also made appointments for when the girls got into town to try on some dresses.

The floral arrangements were made. Omar's mother and grandmother picked the caterer. We only needed our dresses and suits and the venue to complete our big day. I was feeling sick, but I was not about to give in.

Omar started working out with the team. I was at home, feeling sicker and sicker. Every time he called to check on me, I was vomiting. I kept saltine crackers and ginger ale in the truck. I felt like I was neglecting Junior, so I took him Chuck E. Cheese for some fun. We stayed there for two hours. My baby had so much fun. He played video games and ate so much. I was so sick and dizzy at the same time. I had to take care of my baby. Omar checked on us and ended up coming to hang with us. I was happy to see Omar interacting with Junior and to see that Junior liked Omar. I was ready to go home and get into bed, but Omar and Junior went to get ice cream.

Once at home, I couldn't relax because the house phone kept ringing like crazy. Finally, I answered it—it was the paternity results. I called Omar on three-way so we could hear the results together. I felt like I was on Jerry Springer. When it comes to one-month-old Ortiz, Omar, you are not this jigga-boo's father! Praise the Lord! I jumped for joy! I told Omar to hurry up and get home. I wanted to celebrate with him! I opened up a glass of red wine and waited for him to get home. When I heard the car pull up, I ran out to hug Omar. "Damn, baby," he said, "you don't look so good."

"I feel better now."

"I need to take you to the doctor."

"No, Omar, not right now. Let's eat and have a sip of this wine."

"Cool. I'm going to run the little man some bath water and then we need to talk." "Omar, do you hear me?"

"Yes, baby, I do hear you. I'm going to bathe him and you should get comfortable."

We lay down after a long, long day. I was happy to be in his future.

"Tracee, the answer to your question is sixty-five million."

"Sixty-five million what?"

"You asked me about my contract—it's sixty-five million."

"I need to go to bed and process this new information." Friday was getting closer.

My girls all arrived on Friday. Omar's mom came to baby-sit for us. First, we had the fellas meet at the house to get acquainted with my girls. We introduced everybody. Then the ladies got dressed for a night on the town. We took both the Range Rover and the Rolls-Royce. My girls were hitting the club scene in style. We were so sexy; I knew I was. We were so dolled up. I knew some drama was going to go down. Yes, we were ready for it.

I took the girls into the restroom to tell them a little secret. "Hey, y'all, I think I might be having a baby. Please don't tell Omar because I don't know if it's true. So let's just party tonight, and I'll get a test tomorrow. If it's true, I will announce it at dinner tomorrow."

We had a little too much fun. Omar's friends were all over my girls. They couldn't breathe. I knew they liked all the attention. Hell, who wouldn't? We got so sloppy drunk! I could tell that Pedro and Aries really liked each other. They danced all night long. One thing about Spanish men—they will party all night if you let them. By 3:30 AM, all of our feet and toes were hurting. That was our cue to go home. I grabbed Omar, and we loaded up to leave. Everybody was coupled up. All I could say was "Wow!" Everybody was hungry by the time we got back home. I went into the kitchen and made some cold-cuts sandwiches. I started to feel sick again, so I went to bed. Omar shortly followed.

When we woke up the next morning, everybody was still sleep except Momma Velasquez, who was up and ready to go. She whispered in my ear, "I know you're pregnant. Please be careful." I gave her a kiss and told her Omar didn't know yet. "Please don't say anything. I'm going to take the test today. We will call you later."

Chef Peter was cooking Saturday breakfast, so I woke everybody up. They finally all got up to eat. They had satisfied looks on their faces. I didn't know if it was the food or something else. After we all calmed down, I went to look for Omar. He was waiting for me on the chaise in our room. "Have a seat, Tracee."

I did. I told him he might get his wish sooner rather than later. "Omar, I been sick ever since Summer's baby was born. I tried to hide it, but I can't anymore. I'm pregnant."

"*What?*"

"I said I'm pregnant."

He dropped to his knees and kissed my belly. Then he started speaking Spanish to my belly. I knew then that he was happy. He started screaming and jumping around the whole room. Then he called his mom. I knew then it was over. Everybody in Miami would know that we were having a baby. I was grateful that our closest friends were here to share our joy—for the wedding and now, of course, the new baby.

Omar was on cloud nine! He had a lot to celebrate this year—his new contract, his engagement, and his new baby on the way. What a good year! We got dressed so I could go try on dresses with my girls; Omar had his custom-tailored suit company come to the house to measure them for their tuxes.

I went to six different bridal shops. Nothing popped out, but at the last store I found my dress. My girls took pictures and then found their dresses. We were having a great time catching up and talking about last night. Some of them had hooked up with the guys.

I didn't want this weekend to end. I missed my girls and hanging out with them. They missed me, too. We caught up on everything. I needed them here with me, now more than ever. I didn't want them to go. I made them promise to come back way before the wedding.

In getting myself ready for my new life with Omar and the new baby, I knew that I had to tell Junior what was going on. He would not understand, but it was the thought that counted. I sat him down and tried to explain to him that Mommy was going to have a baby.

He smiled like he understood. He gave me a big kiss and touched my stomach and said, "My baby!" I started laughing. I was a proud young momma. My bright young boy seemed to comprehend that the new baby was in my belly.

As the months passed, Omar's career got bigger and better! I felt like I was on top of the world, and I had the right man by my side. My hubby-to-be was happy—as a matter of fact, we all were happy. My belly was nice and round. When Omar came home from work each day, he loved to rub it. He called it his little crystal ball. I was eating so much that I put on twenty-five pounds in less than five months. I was eating everything in sight.

I kept in touch with my girls through e-mail—it was easier that way. They didn't live extravagant lives, but they had real good jobs. They were all educated. I kept them involved in my life so they wouldn't feel left out.

I was surprised to hear that Pedro and Aries still kept in touch with each other and had visited each other since Miami. Aries may have finally met her match—at least for the time being.

Omar was asked to give a speech at a big social event. I couldn't fit into any of my clothes. I didn't want to go this function. I felt like I was so big that if someone stuck a pin on my side, I would burst into little bitty pieces. I was one Super Sonic bacon cheeseburger away from being obese.

Who in his right mind would want to be seen with a "fatty girl" like me? To hear Omar tell it, though, it was so sexy. No matter how much I complained, he loved me unconditionally. I got my ass ready for the social event. Yes, ladies, he was a sweet man—he bought me a dress to wear to the event.

I was moving too slowly, and because Omar didn't want to be late, I told him that I would meet him there. I called Mama Velasquez to watch Junior for the night. I dropped him off at her home; then I drove to the stadium to hear my man speak.

Anyone who has even been in Miami knows that the traffic is ridiculous. I had at least an hour to get there, but the closer I got, the more congested the roads appeared. My phone started to ring like crazy. I grabbed my phone, but it slipped out of my hands. I leaned over to get it, and as I sat up again, I suddenly saw a truck coming right at my car. I tried to swerve out of its way, but it was coming too fast. We hit each other, causing my car to spin out of control. It was the scariest thing that had ever happened to me.

When I woke up, I was in the back of an ambulance. They were asking me so many questions, but I kept blacking out. When I woke up again, I was on an operating table. All I could think about was my unborn child. I could not remember Omar's phone number. I asked where he was, but no one could answer me. I remember a mask being placed over my face—and I was out. I woke up probably several hours later. Omar was sitting on the right side of my hospital bed. He was crying.

"What's wrong?" I asked weakly.

He responded, "You don't know?"

I blinked my eyes and passed out again. When I woke up again, he was holding my hand and kissing it. I didn't know what was going on. My head hurt and my body ached. I went to rub my belly—and that was when I realized that it was gone. I started screaming and yelling at the top of my lungs. I knew something was wrong. I asked Omar, "Where is our baby?"

He started crying really loud. "Mommy, they couldn't save our baby! His lungs weren't fully developed, so he died inside of you. They had to perform an emergency C-section to get the baby out. I held my son for about fifteen minutes. You were on the operating table, and I had to make a choice. They told me they could save your life or try to save his. I didn't want to decide."

"Omar, where is my baby? I need to see him now! *Right now!* Go and get my baby."

The nurse came in and said that she would bring my baby back in. I saw his little hands, feet, and beautiful little features. He was gorgeous. I knew that God had a plan for our stillborn child.

CHAPTER 5

Healing Opportunity

HAD BEEN IN THE HOSPITAL FOR A WEEK. I WASN'T ABLE TO eat. My child was dead. I didn't know if I had killed my baby. Most important, I didn't know how to tell Omar what I could remember before the accident. I was upset with myself.

If I could have changed that tragic day, I would have. I had to address this with Omar when he came to pick me up from the hospital. I was afraid; I hated myself. I was a bad person. How could I explain to my future husband that I was the reason for his baby's death?

Omar arrived and signed off on my release papers. We had to name our baby for hospital records. We decided to call him Deuce Velasquez.

As we drove away from the hospital, I started to cry.

"Don't cry, Tracee, please! We have to be strong for our baby. When it's time, when can try to make another baby."

"Omar, listen to me: I killed our son."

Omar pulled off to the side of the road. "What do you mean?"

"When you called me that day, I dropped my cell phone. I leaned over to pick it up, and the oncoming vehicle smashed right into me. I did try to swerve away, but it was too late. I woke up in an ambulance. And then I woke up again on the operating table, calling your name.

"I can't stomach this right now, Tracee! I can't handle this. I'm going to take you home. I need some time to think."

"What is there to think about, Omar? I told you what happened." The rest of the ride home was quiet. He got out of the car to open my door. I walked slowly into the house, and he drove off, speeding down the street. I called his phone, but when he answered, he started yelling at me.

I hung up. I was already dealing with this, and I couldn't handle Omar's treating me like shit. I went into our room, lay on the bed, and cried until I couldn't cry anymore. I heard Omar pull up in front of the house. He came into the bedroom and started kissing me and crying. He grabbed me around my waist and squeezed me.

"Tracee, I'm sorry. I disrespected you. I need you, baby. I'm really sad, but we are going to get through this. Please don't leave me because of my foolish behavior. I said I wanted to be your husband, and I do. This is a step forward on how to handle problems when they occur. I still will make you my wife. I hope you want the same."

"Of course I do, Omar. I don't want to wait any longer—let's elope right now. Let's go to the justice of the peace and take each other's hand in marriage."

"Okay!"

I couldn't get into the truck fast enough. I had a ring, but Omar didn't. We stopped by his jeweler and picked out a ring; then headed to the justice of the peace.

Pedro and Freddy met us there to be our witnesses. We made them promise not to tell until Valentine's Day of next year. We still were having the wedding, but the tragedy of our son's death pushed us closer to marriage.

The ceremony was quick and simple. I do, I do, I do, I do, and that was it. I now pronounce you husband and wife; you may kiss the bride. We did exactly that. Then I was ready to go home and lie down. This was a very good thing to do. My life was moving forward. I was now Mrs. Tracee Velasquez. Don't get it twisted—I was ready to be wifey, but I still wanted a wedding, too. We could start all over again, but now we were a complete couple. I needed to rest for about a week. I had to plan funeral arrangements for our baby. This was truly the hardest thing to do, but I had to do it. I went to the funeral home and picked out a small powder blue casket. I had an artist paint a picture of me and Omar holding our son on the inside of the coffin. It was beautiful, like our baby boy. I had programs printed for the funeral, having set the date for the following Saturday to give my family and friends time to prepare for such a sad occasion.

I was at peace with myself. I'd stopped blaming myself. I was a firm believer that everything happens for a reason. I put it in the Lord's hands. My baby was in heaven.

When I got home, I passed out on the bed. I must have slept for at least four hours. My mother-in-law showed up with Junior, who seemed happy to see me. Omar came home about ten minutes later, and Momma Velasquez prepared some dinner for us. I had no energy to get up and do anything. I gave my husband a kiss and took a shower. The stitches were itching.

I went downstairs to talk with Omar and his mother. "Hey, guys, I finished all of the funeral arrangements. We will have the service next Saturday at noon. I'm waiting to hear back from my family." Omar started crying. I walked over to give him a hug. We all started crying. I called my spiritual mother to help us through this tough time in our lives. She prayed for us. We all felt better after she blessed our souls and minds. She helped change the mood from bad to good.

We sat down to dinner—Momma Velasquez had cooked a huge meal. We had tacos, enchiladas, and rice with refried beans. Afterward, I put my son to bed. Omar and his mom stayed up all night, talking, while I went to sleep.

I got up early the next morning. I needed to go shopping for clothes to wear for the funeral. As I was out I got a disturbing phone call from Pooky. He was calling me to tell me that Aries had been hospitalized. I was so nervous for her, I couldn't even focus on my own tragedy. We were best friends. I called her mother to find out what the hell was wrong with her. Aries had been diagnosed with congestive heart failure. She was on oxygen.

I talked to her mother for three hours. I told her mom, "If she overcomes this, I am going to move her out here with me. If any change occurs with Aries, please call me." I was really going through a lot. My baby's funeral was approaching, and my best friend was ill.

I called Omar to tell him the bad news. He wanted to meet me for lunch to help calm me down. We met up at a little Cuban restaurant. I was shaking and totally worn out. My husband showed up with flowers and love. He could see how much I was hurting. It was affecting me physically—my face was breaking out, I was losing weight, and my hair was falling out. I was losing my freaking mind. "Omar, after this is over, I need a real vacation, away from everybody. I want to go to a retreat to relax my mind, body, and soul."

"Yes, baby, we can do that. I will make arrangements. I can take a leave of up to three days."

"Do you promise? Omar, I need this time to spend with you. I'll make arrangements to have Junior watched. All I need from you is the okay to book the trip."

"Let's get through this funeral, and we can go from there."

"Also, if Aries get well, I want to know if I can move her out here with us. She needs me, and I need to be there for her. Today was a bad day." I felt like my faith was being tested every day. I started reading my Bible. I knew I could at least count on the Bible to get me through these tough times. I made a promise to myself to read at least one scripture every day. I did just that.

Before the wake, I had to take my baby's clothes to the funeral parlor. This was the hardest part to prepare for. When I got home, I grabbed my Bible and read until I fell asleep. Omar was home when I woke up. "What are you doing up this early?" "Baby, I couldn't sleep. I'm sad and happy at the same time. I just want to get through today, and I think I will be fine."

I got up and got dressed; I got Junior ready also. We ate some breakfast and shed some tears. This morning would be long. I went to check on Omar. He was on his knees, praying, so I didn't disturb him. I waited patiently for my husband. He gave me a look that I had never seen before in my life, a look of ease, maybe even forgiveness. I was happy to get any reaction from him. I hated silence.

Omar kissed me then—it was so passionate. I had to face both families and see my dead baby in a casket. The limo was waiting for us. It was time to leave. The drive to the funeral home felt so long.

Deuce had a lot of family support at his funeral. I felt like I had done a good job planning this funeral. Everything was going to be beautiful. I knew even though this was a sad occasion that everybody would make it to the end.

I was surprised to see how many of my husband's co-workers attended. There were so many cars and people in line. My family was escorted in first; Omar's family was next. After everyone else was seated, the aisle was cleared for Omar and I to walk in and be seated. People started screaming and hollering as soon as we walked in. I got so upset. It was our baby's funeral, but people were drawing so much attention to themselves that the focus was not on us anymore. How rude! I hadn't begun to let it all out when some woman I didn't even know decided to pass out at my baby's funeral.

I know it was rude, but I leaned over to one of the church ushers and asked for the woman to be removed. She was just too damn hysterical for me. This is not an audition for the most dramatic woman at a funeral, especially not here, right now.

The woman was one of the first people to be removed. The pastor gave his condolences to the families and gave a warm and thoughtful blessing to all of us. Suddenly, I heard men yelling right behind me. Omar turned around and asked them take their disruptive discussion outside immediately. Both men paused, as if they didn't realize they were louder than the preacher—and they started cussing out Omar.

It became a chain reaction. Luckily, the police also were there to assist. I stood up—enough was enough. This was supposed to be a time for mourning; it quickly was becoming "Who can talk louder than the preacher?" I was so ready to get everyone out of the church. I told the usher that if there was one more loud outbreak, they should ask everybody to leave. Omar and I didn't need anything else to happen.

As usual, I put my foot in my mouth. People lined up to view the baby and that was when all hell officially broke loose. They started pushing the person in front of them, and a fight broke out—a fight right in front of our eyes. I couldn't believe this shit. A fight at a funeral. The worst of it all was they were in front of the coffin, and someone must have stumbled as the police were grabbing people, and the coffin closed shut!

I fell to my knees. I was screaming, "Get everyone out!" Omar was yelling the same thing. The police cleared the entire church. We were so upset and sad. I was shocked and pissed off. I didn't expect anything like this to happen, not in my wildest dreams.

We finished up the services, and the pallbearers entered to bring our baby out. We followed shortly after. Reporters from the news stations were all outside, waiting. I felt like this would be broadcast all over Miami. People were lined up, giving interviews. I refused to even look at a camera crew. After that fiasco in the church, we asked for only the immediate family to be present at the cemetery. Omar was so well respected that everyone agreed to our wishes. This was our last time to say our good-byes to the baby. My mother and Omar's mother started crying like crazy, hollering and crying at the top of their lungs.

I looked behind me and saw everybody leaving and walking to their cars. Thank God! I wanted some alone time so I could have a peace of mind. Omar just held my hands. He would not let go.

My husband was really emotional. I knew he would need all of my attention and support. I was willing to do whatever I had to do. I was in it for the long haul. We placed our roses onto the coffin and left.

The drive back to the house seemed extremely long. Omar cried the whole way there. It made me cry, too. Everyone was waiting for us at the house—I didn't even know half of the people in our home. There was so much food, but I didn't want to eat a thing. I was exhausted. This entire day was upsetting to the both of us. I said my hellos and goodbyes. I needed to lie down. I went upstairs, and I was out for the night.

I got up and took a bath. It was relaxing. Omar came and got in with me. We cried together. I washed my man's body. It released some tension off of him. He fell asleep in my arms. I woke him up to get out and go to bed.

We'd accomplished our goal by staying strong and making an active lifestyle as a high-priority couple living in today's society. All we had was each other to get through this tough time. The best attitude could get us far in anything we put our minds to.

It now was time to move on. There was nothing we could change. Now, we only could improve ourselves. It was time to start fresh. I waited for everybody to go back home so we get our lives back on track. One by one, they started leaving. Last but not least were our friends. They didn't want to leave. I assured them we were fine, that it was okay for them to leave. They respected our wishes.

A new time was coming. We had to get ready and back on track. Omar went back to work. I made some phone calls to get myself together—my massage therapist, my beautician, and our chef.

I was ready for a new look. I wanted to have a life-changing experience. I felt this was the only way for me to redeem my womanhood. I had plans, and I was only hoping for the best results.

I felt that once I got a response from the important family members that I could move on to the next chapter in life. I need a new goal for myself. I even thought about maybe writing a novel. I thought about becoming a model. Anything was possible.

CHAPTER 6

Beauty Calls

S WOMEN THERE ARE ONLY A FEW THINGS WE NEED TO put a pep in our step—a good massage, a great cook, a new outfit, and of course, a new hairdo! As women, we also have to remember to take care of ourselves and to always look our best, no matter what. You never know when an opportunity might present it self.

Omar was gone, and I wanted a makeover. I needed some "me" time. I felt like this would be an all-day event, so I called my mother-in-law over to watch Junior, and off to the spa I went.

I went to my massage therapist first. I got a hot-rock massage. It helped to relieve stress and relax my body muscles. This normally was a ninety-minute session. I had gone through a lot recently, so this was just the new beginning I needed for the new change in my life.

Next I wanted a rejuvenating facial. This helped with fine lines and wrinkles. As we know, "black don't crack." I like this facial because it also helps cleanse the skin of acne, blackheads, and uneven skin tones. This session usually lasts one hour, twenty-five minutes.

The day started off great. I finished the most difficult spa treatments and would next get a manicure and pedicure. This nail tech at the spa was a celebrity nail tech; she has traveled with best of the best, showing off her skills. This session was another two hours. Aneeda Richman, my nail tech, usually put me to sleep during my time with her. I liked her a lot. She was a good listener. I didn't mind her prices at all—a good nail tech was hard to find. I wrapped up my session with her and paid for my other services at the spa. It now was time to get to the hair salon.

My beautician was one of the best I have had in a long time. He would be very surprised by the service that I would request from him. He is a diva, and I love him to death. This was a gossip shop—my stylist does get all the news on everybody. The drama would start as soon as I walked in.

I walked in, and he started immediately: "Bitch, what is this I hear that people was fighting at your baby's funeral?" I paused for a second, and then I told him everything that happened. He laughed for a good twenty minutes.

"Jerome, I did not come to relive that day. I got something I want you to do with my hair."

"Like what?"

"Cut it all off of my head. Like, I want a short cut. A really short cut. No exceptions, Jerome."

"Everybody, listen up. Tracee has lost her damn mind! I knew you looked funny coming in here today, but I will not cut your hair. Omar will not send any of his head-hunting family after me."

"Diva, you don't have to worry about it at all. Do it, or I will find someone who will."

"Oh, so now you're complicated, and you want to get crazy because you are going through some shit. Okay, bitch, I will cut it all off, but if Omar comes after me, it will be your ass that I will kick."

"Jerome, just cut it, and we will deal with him later. I want a new me. I'm trying to change myself and start off fresh and new. Help me, please!"

"I'm going to cut it off, and excuse me, madam, do you want to save this hair or let it be?"

"Save it! I want to remember this day."

It was done. It was cute! It was short! It was really all cut off. I loved it! Jerome did the damn thang on my hair. Omar would be surprised, but he would like my new haircut. I got so many compliments on my hair that Jerome asked me to do a photo shoot.

I gladly accepted his offer. I had a feeling that this would be a great opportunity for the both us—exposure for me and more exposure for Jerome. He didn't need his head to get any bigger than it already was. We set up the date for the photo shoot, and I left for the mall to get some new clothes. I bought a couple of pairs of jeans with sexy tops. I bought some new pumps. I even found some cute dresses. People started approaching me from left and right about my hair. I knew it was cute, but dang!

All kinds of men were hitting on me and making passes at me—I think a few women, too! This was hilarious. This was a great makeover—my new haircut and new clothes and shoes. All I needed was some jewelry to complete my new look.

I called to check on my baby boy. He was napping. I called Omar, but he did not answer. I thought he was maybe off the field, so I left a message. I was leaving the mall when Omar returned my phone call. I wanted to meet him for dinner. He agreed, and I ran home to get changed for my dinner date. Omar was excited to see my new look. I didn't tell him anything. I told him that he would not be mad, and I would see him in an hour.

I got home and my first critics were Junior and Momma Velasquez. She fell in love with my new look. I showed her all my new clothes and told her about the photo shoot next week. She was pleased and very happy for me. I asked her to stay a little longer so that Omar and I could have dinner. I wore some tight, skinny jeans with a low-cut shirt. All I needed was my pumps to finish this look. I was too cute! I couldn't wait to see Omar.

I kissed Junior and Momma, and then I left. I pulled up at our favorite dinner spot. Omar didn't see me drive up. I walked past him, and he still didn't recognize me. Finally, I tapped him on his shoulder. He slapped me on my butt and pulled me closer to him and gave me a big sloppy kiss.

"Damn, baby, you look so good! I love your haircut. I really like this new look." He paused for a second and smiled and kissed me again. "Babe, this is turning me on!" I was excited that Omar was digging this new look. I didn't know what kind of reaction to expect from him. I loved it! We ordered some appetizers and a few drinks. He was all smiles all night. "Babe, I love your look! I really do love it!"

"Omar, there is something I want to talk to you about. Jerome asked me to be in a photo shoot next week. I said yes. How do you feel about me doing the shoot?"

"Do it. I think this is a great opportunity for you to strut your stuff."

"Then it is settled. I will do the photo shoot."

"What did you do today?"

"I went to the spa for about six hours. Then I spent another two hours with Jerome at the salon. I also went to the mall to get some outfits to wear at the photo shoot. I'm excited to do this, and maybe if the pictures come out good, a magazine might want to publish my pictures."

"That sounds great, T. I'm so proud of you. I'm glad I married babe. I'm so glad."

We drank so much at dinner. I was actually glad to get some time alone with Omar. I needed this, and he did as well. We enjoyed each other's company. We ordered dinner, and Omar stared at me all night long. He had the biggest smile on his sexy face. He undressed me with his eyes. I made him wait until we got home. We talked about a whole bunch of nothing. Omar was ready to go home for hard sex. I wasn't really ready yet—after all, he might mess up my hair.

The whole ride home, all I could think about was Omar's facial expression when he saw my haircut. I was thrilled. I was happy, too. Omar made me feel like a sexy woman all the time.

We arrived home. Momma Velasquez was ready to go. Omar kissed his mother good-bye. Junior was asleep. It was late, and Omar had to get up for work tomorrow. They had a big game tomorrow. I knew exactly what to do to get him ready for his big day. This was going to be a long night.

I did all the tricks he liked. He didn't require as much as usual. Good for me! I was tired as hell after the damn running around I'd done today. Omar was fast asleep. I went to take a bath. I lit my candles and relaxed in the tub for about an hour.

I read a couple of scriptures in the Bible and went to sleep. I had a long day ahead of me tomorrow as well. I wanted to take Junior to the park and the toy store. I also wanted to scope out a few Montessori schools for him. It was getting time for him to get in school and interact with other kids his age.

The chef arrived to cook us breakfast the next morning. Omar was on a strict diet, so he refused to let me cook during the season. I didn't mind at all. I was able to do other things around the house.

I called Jerome and told him the good news. He was happy; I was even happier. I asked him, "Could you suggest some colors that you prefer me to wear?"

He replied, "You are a diva like me, so stick with the season trends and colors, and we will make it happen." Okay, diva, then I will see you in a couple of days. I sat and watched Junior play with other kids at the park for a couple of hours. He did pretty well. He didn't punch any kids, but he did punk a few of them. That was the icing on the cake to see that in full action. I didn't find any schools that caught my eye. I would continue until I found what I was looking for. Until then, Junior would be with me every day.

The day had gone so fast. I had to get us ready for Omar's game that night. I gave Junior a bath, and I got ready also. We ate a quick snack and then drove to the stadium. I really didn't want to drive, but I didn't have enough time to arrange for a ride with another player's wife. I was running a bit behind schedule. I knew we would make it there on time, and we did.

We ran to our seats and cheered the team all the way to victory. It was good win. We went down to the family area. Omar came out to greet us. I'd been happy to see him play. He looked so good in his uniform.

"Babe, I need to change my clothes, so give me about twenty minutes, and I'll be right out."

I sat and chatted with some of the other wives. Junior ran over to play with their kids. I watched him interact with other kids his age. As I was watching my son, a group of females was watching me. I could see them turning their heads as they walked through the benches. I paused and gave them something to look at. I giggled and strutted to the end of family area. I didn't know who they were. They either knew Omar or me, but I didn't care. I waited and then decided to introduce myself to these women. I did just that. I walked my country ass right over.

"Hello, my name is Tracee Velasquez. How are you ladies doing this evening?" I needed to be the bigger woman. After all, I didn't know them, but I made sure they knew me. I carried a fake conversation, just to waste time. Omar was ready to go after signing autographs from some of the other kids in the area. I was curious as to who these woman belonged to. The last thing on my mind was if they were there for Omar. Our relationship was wrapped tight. Omar would be a fool to cheat on me. I was no dummy. I wouldn't open Pandora's box if I didn't have to.

We went home for our relaxing couple of days off, leaving one of the vehicles there at the stadium. I just didn't want to drive home; I wanted to leave as a family. We drove home. Omar's phone started ringing like crazy. I told him to answer it.

"Babe, I will answer it later. It's not important. I'm spending time with you. I can return the phone calls when we get home. Let's enjoy this drive home. Let's enjoy some relaxing music."

I was too concerned about those chicken-heads at the stadium. I couldn't figure out if it was my women's intuition or if I was just tripping. Nevertheless, I felt how I felt. I was a woman. *Get it together!* I was ready for anything and everything that came my way. Ladies, don't get it twisted. Once Omar went to sleep, I would do what I had to do: I would checking his mutha-fucking phone.

Fuck that! I would go through his phone ASAP! I couldn't wait. I was impatient, and he was taking his precious time with going to bed. If this fool didn't hurry up, I would get pissed. After two long hours of anticipation, it was finally time to get down and dirty. I grabbed his phone and went directly into the bathroom and locked the door. *Let's see what I can find.* I decided to start with his text messages. I went through thirty messages. First of all, I found nothing—I mean, nothing at all. I got upset and hoped that I was not jumping to conclusions. I didn't care. I needed to go with my gut feelings. My guts didn't lie. I then looked through all of his missed calls. I found six of the same number, with no name attached to it. I looked at how many times this number had appeared—it showed up at least twelve times but on different days.

I wasn't alarmed. I wrote down all the numbers that didn't have names to them. I decided to return the call. I was totally shocked to hear the voice on the other end of my hubby's line.

It was a female. I hung up! I paused for a second to get my head together. I was about to call her back when she called me. I did what any woman would do in this situation: I answered it.

"Who is this?" she asked.

My eyes got so big. I replied, "Who the hell is *this*, and what do want?"

"I would like to speak with Omar."

"Who?"

"I said, I would like to speak with Omar."

"What do you want with my husband?" I asked.

"I feel this is none of your business, and if I wanted to talk to you, then I would have called you instead of your husband."

Oh, no, this *bitch* did not go there! I was a second away from being crazy, and now this hood-rat wanted to challenge my place in my relationship with my husband. She'd better hope that I didn't locate her ass! No, better yet, I would find her on GP! That's gangster talk! She was about to bring the hood out of me. This was something I didn't want Omar to know about me, but what the hell! At this point, I didn't give a damn.

She kept calling back, and I cussed her out every time she called. I got tired of her and her calls. I decided to listen to what she had to say. I checked her first. After I checked her monkey ass, then I was ready to listen. She didn't want a thing. She called herself a friend and said that she was checking on him because she knew about the funeral. I was very mad about her knowing about my baby's funeral. I listened, but I really wasn't hearing a damn thing she had to say. I told her good night and that was it. That's what I got for snooping around. I felt I had every right to do what I did. I wasn't ashamed of what I did if Omar found out. If I had to answer to him, then it was what it was. Omar might have brought home the check, but I ran this house. Let the truth be told, he wasn't home long enough to dirty it anyway. As a matter of fact, I wasn't even home enough either, but enough to put dirty dishes in the sink, and let the maid in, and return to watch her leave.

Life is filled with unexpected trials and tribulations. As a woman, you just have to deal with it the best way you can. As for me, I loved to go face first and ask questions later. I set myself up for whatever.

I calmed down enough to go to bed. I turned off Omar's phone and put it back where I'd found it. Omar rolled over as I got into bed and said some words that caught me off guard: "So did you talk to Tatum? I heard you in the bathroom, so I assumed you were going through my phone anyway."

"Well, yes I did. She wasn't talking about anything that I wanted to hear. She tried to tell me that y'all were friends. I didn't care to hear that. I also wanted to know why she kept calling your phone so much. She didn't have an answer. Basically, I checked her and gave her a chance to explain herself. I felt enough was enough, and I ended the entire conversation. Omar, as your wife, you have to expect me to uncover and find out things that I feel you are keeping a secret from me. If it isn't a secret and if you don't have anything to hide, then this should never be a problem if I go through your phone. I not ashamed of what I did. To be honest with you, I will continue to do it if I feel like you're lying to me. I trust you baby! Please don't be upset with me."

Omar looked at me, rolled back over, and didn't say a word. I tapped him on his shoulder, but he ignored me. I was mad—but not mad. I went downstairs to have a drink of wine. I ended up drinking the entire bottle. When I woke up, it was morning. The bottle was on the floor next to me by the couch. All I could do was laugh! I couldn't believe myself. I hoped this wasn't the start of something that I couldn't end.

I call myself making him dinner to make up for roaming through his phone. He liked me to look sexy, so I did, of course. I slaved all day long, preparing a hot meal. I waited patiently for him to get home, watching the clock for about three hours. It was getting late. This man was not home. I couldn't imagine that he was mad at me! This wasn't anything to be mad about. This is just a step of being committed to a relationship and trying to have some type of trust with each other. I felt I'd done nothing wrong.

My husband did not walk through the door. I fed Junior and gave him a bath; then cleaned up my mess from cooking dinner. As I was putting the delicious food into Tupperware containers, Omar pulled up. I ran to the door and questioned him.

"Don't raise your voice, Tracee! I went out with some sponsors for dinner. I didn't need you to be there, so I didn't tell you. I was and still will be very mad at you. I don't care that you slaved over a hot stove and cooked me a gourmet dinner."

My left eyebrow raised, and that was it! I went the fuck off on him. "Omar, please don't make me think that because I went through your phone that you were that mad at me. Please come up with a better damn excuse than that. I'm sure you have had worse things happen than something as simple as this. Omar, people have done way worse things to you. I don't believe you. I honestly don't believe that this would make you act out like this. Please get a grip! You really need to get a clue and then find your own damn answer. I am not stuck on stupid, so don't try to manipulate me. I'm going to bed. I'm now officially mad at you, Omar. You can sleep in the guest room." I ran a bath, and played some soft music, and sipped a glass of wine.

Omar ran upstairs and threw a fit. I didn't give damn. I ignored him and put on my pajamas to go to bed. I guess he thought I was playing with him. He tried to get in bed with me. "Leave me alone tonight," I said. Oh, my goodness, why had I said that? He really started tripping. Omar cussed and yelled at me. I rolled over so that he was yelling at a wall because I wasn't paying him any attention. He yelled for about twenty minutes. I was laughing on the inside, but I kept my mean face on the outside.

This was going to be a long night. I felt like he was trying to make me mad. I wasn't about to let him get under my skin. I had to prepare myself for my photo shoot in three days. Omar stayed mad at me for another two days himself.

The day had arrived! It was now time to get my sexy on. The world wasn't ready for my pictures and me. I called Jerome to confirm my hair appointment and the photo shoot. Everything was intact. There was nothing to keep me from this terrific day. I was so prepared.

I got my outfits pressed. I grabbed all of my accessories and shoes and lip gloss and put everything into my duffle bag. I called Junior's nanny—she was already on her way to our home.

As soon as Ms. Olga arrived, I gave my baby a kiss and ran out the front door. I called Jerome to tell him to meet me at the shop. I got there before Jerome, and as I waited for him, I heard a woman's voice that sounded familiar. I thought for a second and then realized who it was.

I was about to approach her when Jerome strolled through the front door. He loved to make an appearance. I laughed, and so did everybody else. "Hey, Miss Thing, are you ready for the shoot?"

"Yes, I am, sir. Yes I am!"

"Let's get it started, diva."

I was getting my hair washed when all of a sudden, Omar walked through the door. I wrapped my hair in a towel, and he escorted me right outside. He started going off on me and yelled for a long time.

All I could do was stare at him. After he stopped yelling, it was time for me to talk. "Omar, why are you here? I left the house while you were sleeping. I didn't tell you good-bye or even say a word to you. I left, and that was that."

"Tracee, you knew I was still mad at you, and—"

"Omar, I didn't owe you an explanation about why I called homegirl back. I did what I did. I don't care. Omar, all of this could have been eliminated if you would have talked to her when she called you. Deal with it! It's done and over with. I have moved on. I tried to clear the tension between us, but all you did was escalate it even more. I'm not going to kiss your ass. I left it alone; I was done trying to kiss and make up with you.

"So because you feel that I didn't tell you—or better yet, remind you—of my photo shoot today, you think I was tripping. Whatever! Omar, you really need to get a grip, and get it together. I'm not one of these whores that you were use to dealing with. I'm your wife. I have feelings. I'm a person with standards. I have morals that I live by every day. I felt like you did, too! Apparently not, Omar. You are changing for worse, not better. I need to get back in and finish. I will call you as soon as I get done."

Omar left. I knew he was mad at me still, but I had other obligations. I was there to get some exposure, and I needed to fully focus on me for once. Jerome finished my hair, and it was now time to get going with the photo shoot.

I got dressed, and my hair and outfit coordinated so well. The photographer was so impressed with me that she asked me to do another shoot the very next day. She said I took great pictures. She assured me that I would get some calls about doing more shoots soon.

I was happy. I couldn't thank both Jerome and Peggy, the photographer, enough. I left with a huge smile on my face. Omar and I were fighting, but I still got the job done today. I called my hubby to tell him the wonderful news. I talked to him until I got home. I sat down at the dinner table, and we talked for several hours. We laid everything out—our likes and dislikes that we do to each other. Finally, after a long discussion, it was over.

Omar wanted to know about my photo shoot. I told him that they wanted to send my pictures to a couple of agencies. I allowed them to do it. Also I told him that they wanted me to do another shoot tomorrow. I agreed to do another, too.

He was excited for me. We ate dinner, and it had been such a long day that I fell asleep fast. I woke up and got dressed. Omar decided to take Junior to hang out while I did my shoot. I told him that I would meet up with them a little later.

I arrived at Peggy's studio to do the shoot. Jerome was waiting for me. He restyled my hair, and we choose a couple of outfits to wear. My makeup was flawless. I was so sexy. I knew this was going to be great. Peggy asked me how I felt about modeling.

"I've always wanted to model," I answered.

"I have a friend who works for a huge black magazine company," she told me. "It's called *Play-Toy* magazine—it's bigger than *Playboy!*" She wanted to send my photos over immediately. "I can't guarantee a job for you, but I'll try."

I was excited just to be considered. I signed some release papers for the photos, and as I was about to leave, Peggy's phone started ringing.

It was a representative from *Play-Toy* magazine. They wanted to know who I was and how soon they could set up a meeting with me. I was in total shock. My pictures were sent over, and within twenty minutes they we ready to meet me.

I called Omar and told him to come to the photography studio. Omar pulled me aside—he wanted to know if I really wanted to do this. He said he would support me 100 percent.

"I am ready," I told him. "Yes, I want to do it."

I spoke with a representative named Melissa. She was going to be my contact person for the magazine. We exchanged phone numbers and e-mail addresses. I didn't know what to expect, but I was ready for whatever. Omar was, too!

"Baby, I'm proud of you! I hope you're ready for fame of your own."

"Yep! I'm ready. It's time to do what I gotta do!"

CHAPTER 7

All Eyes on T

ODAY WAS THE BIG MEETING WITH MELISSA. I HADN'T BEEN able to sleep all weekend. I got one of my baddest skirt sets and fully put my outfit together. They were not ready for the diva to walk through the door. I took my time to get dressed. I put my makeup on with perfection. I knew I was so ready for today. I drove to the building where the meeting was set and checked in with the receptionist. She told me to have a seat and that Melissa was expecting me.

I was nervous and texted Omar the entire time I was waiting. I couldn't believe I was finally here. I knew that I needed to make a good impression. I wanted this job so bad. I made sure that I was punctual and that I spoke clearly.

Melissa called me into her office. I took a deep breath and then walked in. There were three other people in room with us. I shook their hands, and then we got right down to business. I was comfortable being around them.

They got to know me and offered me a three-year contract on the spot. Wow! I guess I impressed them. I was offered $500,000 the first year, with a travel bonus of $100,000. The second year I would get $1,000,000m with a travel bonus of $150,000. My third year with the magazine, I would receive $2,500,000, with no travel bonus but with incentives that could range up to $1,000,000.

Could a girl ask for anything else? I was excited. I sent over the contract to our attorney—I was allowed one week to make a decision. I really wanted my attorney to look over the contract in case I might have missed something in the clause.

Everything was pretty clear-cut. No hidden surprises. After a couple of days I went back to Melissa with a signed contract. I was totally prepared to start my photo sessions.

Everything was coming into play. Omar and I were happy again. We'd made up. I had a job. I was living my dream. I was getting paid. Can you say money, money, money? I started getting job offers like crazy. I was under contract with *Play-Toy*, though, so I couldn't accept any other jobs.

I told them even though I was contracted under *Play-Toy* that I would contact them. I was quite sure that they knew they would have to pay me top dollar. I was very enthusiastic about taking pictures—getting paid was just icing on the cake.

I got my first check—all of those zeros! I felt like this check was just the very beginning to my new life. All eyes were on me now! There were two stars in house.

Omar loved the attention that I got from strangers. There wasn't much focus on him anymore. Jealousy never crossed my mind, nor did it cross Omar's. It was amazing how fast a month had gone by.

I had my own income. I was meeting the big dogs of the company. I had to make guest appearances and sign books. This was definitely the life I'd always wanted for myself—true fame and my own fortune.

Omar's career was at an ultimate high. He was getting endorsement deals that were out of this world. We decided to just sit back and watch the money roll in. I was offered a book deal. The book company was interested in my life experiences. Of course, I was not ready to tell all just yet. I can't deny the fact that I wanted to do the deal, but I knew I had plenty of time a little later. I was the hottest thing going. *Play-Toy* knew it. I had interviews to do. Public speaking required me to have an assistant. I was too proud to hire one, so the company hired one for me.

I was moving at such a fast pace. Instead of one foot in front of the other, it felt like two feet at the same time. My assistant had booked me so many jobs during the week that it was taken time away from Junior, which I did not like at all. I ordered my assistant to get me a baby-sitter for all studio jobs.

In my contract there wasn't a clause that said my child was restricted from the premises. I did what any mother would do in such a case: I brought him with me. My assistant watched my son during my shoots.

Everything was coming into play. Omar was happier than ever. He was able to see me shine like the star that I was. This life was going to be a true challenge in our relationship. It was either going to change for better or just get worse. Whatever the case, I was going to be ready. Omar called me to propose a photo together. His agent thought this would be great publicity for the both of us—he as a high-paid athlete and me as the upcoming highly requested model.

I called Melissa to discuss it with her. She also agreed that this would bring in more revenue for everyone. So we quickly signed on the dotted line. Our pictures turned out nice—we looked like we were a match made in heaven. That was exactly what they wanted. We needed this. I knew at that moment that we were on our way to the top! A real family photo would catch America's eye. They picked the perfect three for it.

Melissa felt it was time to celebrate the big launch of the photographs debut. We set a time and a place to meet with editors and the rest of the staff. Melissa picked a really expensive restaurant to have dinner. We met at Chef Le Brouff, an Italian-family–owned upscale restaurant.

I made sure we dressed to impress. I put on a sexy Gucci fitted two-piece skirt set that complemented my figure. I mean, it really did just that. This outfit hugged every curve that I had. Omar put on one of his tailor-made suits, from Gucci also.

We coordinated well. We considered ourselves the Mr. and Mrs. Trump of fashion! We loved making fashion statements. It was time to make things happen. We arrived at the venue and greeted everyone. We sat down and went right to business.

Melissa told us that this photo would be in all the top magazines. The only thing we had to do was sign all the rights over and agree to the release of the pictures. So I asked her a question: "If we release the rights to these pictures, does that mean you guys can sell them to the highest bidder?"

"Not exactly," she replied. "We can let the magazines bid for the pictures they want first, then sell the rights to them, and then we can profit from them like that."

Wow! I felt like Brad Pitt and Angelina Jolie—they were the gurus of paid photos. I getting a little too pumped up about this whole deal. I asked to be excused from the table so that Omar and I could discuss if this was something that we wanted to do. I also had to remind him that this was a part of life now, so if he didn't want the public in our home life that we should just say no right now.

He said he comfortable with it and that we should do it. We walked back to the table, thanked everyone for coming, and signed all the rights over to Melissa. She was excited—maybe even a little more than we were. America was going to meet the Velasquez family.

A whole month went by and to our surprise, the very first photo was on the cover of *Play-Toy* magazine. In following days, we started seeing ourselves on *Ebony*, *Jet*, and *Essence* magazines. We were big-timers now! People recognized me more than ever.

I was nervous—I didn't want anyone to put me in an uncomfortable spot. I called everybody back in Las Vegas and told them to go pick up any magazines with Omar and me on them. We had total family support. I got phone calls left and right.

Melissa called us with some great news. One of the biggest talk-show hosts wanted us to appear on her show. Tiffany was taping a show about black women dating outside their race and getting married. The twist to the episode was that these were famous professional athletes, actors, activists, models, film directors, etc. She thought that this would be a great publicity for the both of us.

I told her that I needed to talk to Tiffany about this. In the back of mind, all I could think of was that we were going on Tiffany's show! It didn't get better than that. She was the queen of all talk-show hosts. What better way to advertise anything new that I was trying to do?

I went to the fabric store and bought some fabric to sew onto my boots. I decided to change up and design some outfits to wear on her show. I knew that once she saw my designs that she would want to hire me to design some clothes for her. I got right down to business.

I had a natural knack for designing clothes and also had a true passion for it. I was in the zone. I put together some of the baddest outfits—I knew exactly what to do. I was ready for business.

It took me a day to convince Omar and a week to put together a jacket, a pair of dress slacks, and some designer boots. I knew if I wore this outfit on the show that the entire world would see it. This would be great business for my new adventure into bringing home some more money.

Melissa called us to verify flight arrangements and hotel accommodations. We set up a meeting and a limo drop-off and pick-up. We had three other magazines shoots set up, too. Omar was amazed by my assertiveness in putting all this together. My dreams were starting to come true, and I was taking full responsibility.

Momma Velasquez came to watch Junior, and off we went To Chi-town. This was going to the best trip ever. I had my man by my side. He was letting me take full charge of this mission. After we landed, we and went straight to our first shoot. *Let's rock and roll!* We were tired, but we still looked good on film.

This shoot required us to pose with some nudity. I was topless and sat in his lap with my arms wrapped around him. Omar was sexy. All you could see was my back with his arms wrapped around my body. *Sexy! Sexy! Sexy!*

We were there for two hours and then checked in at the hotel. We had a note from Tiffany's management. They wanted to go out to dinner. I looked at the time—we had less than forty-five minutes to get ready. They got to see me with my bare face—I mean, no makeup, no eyelashes, no nothing. I was embarrassed, but I really didn't care. I was happy to be in the same place as Tiffany. I had so many questions for her. I wore one of my outfits—compliments, compliments, nothing but compliments all night long. All I was waiting for was the big question.

She asked, "Can you design me a couple of pairs of boots and jackets."

I told her it was consignment designing. I asked for old clothes and shoes. This was the only way to get what she wanted. Tiffany agreed, and she had her assistant deliver a bag of goodies to our hotel room later that evening.

I packed a bag and read over some questions that would be asked on her show. I couldn't sleep—I was anxious but happy. I was going on a big talk show. I told all of my family and friends that we would be taping the show tomorrow.

Omar gave the look of lust. We made love all night long. I was so tired, but I was so ready for the show. The limo was waiting outside the next morning to take us to the studio. When we arrived for hair and makeup, my shit was flawless. Omar was stunning, as always. The power couple was ready for their debut.

We sat on the panel with big-timers: Michael Bordan, Coby Giant, Haqeel O'Neal, Leopard Woods. The list went on and on. I had to admit that I was the prettiest wife on the panel. I could feel the jealousy. I didn't care; I already knew I was going to be the hot one!

We all were asked a series of questions:

1. How did you meet your spouse?
2. What was your career before you became a wife?

3. Did you know that you would be with your mate?
4. How many children, if any, do you have with each other?
5. What are your future plans?
6. What are the up and downs of being a spotlight wife?

There were seven wives answering questions. I smiled and kept my composure every time I had to answer my questions. I spoke clearly and was very professional. Later, we took questions from the audience. I liked the questions I was asked and answered them completely. I didn't get too many smart-mouth responses.

After the taping ended, Omar kissed me and told me I'd done a wonderful job. I gave Tiffany my direct contact information for her clothes and shoes and told her that it would take me two weeks to complete my work.

Omar was hungry, so he and I decided to go to dinner. I was hoping for some Jamaican food. We wanted to eat something different. The limo driver took us to a hole-in-the-wall called Yosemite's. This was some good food. I ate so much that my stomach hurt. One thing about Jamaican food is that it is filling.

Back at the hotel, I put our clothes together for the next shoot—an outside shoot. The forecast called for bad weather, which pissed me off. My hair would be messed up; I knew it. I just knew it.

Before I went to bed, I got down on my knees and prayed. I prayed so hard that I was crying tears of joy. Tears of happiness. God was on my side. I knew he was watching over my family and our lives. I got up and took a relaxing bath. The next morning, I knew it would be a good day after all—the weather was not ugly.

Omar put on denim, provided by Prada, with some Gucci sneakers. I liked this sleek look. Omar had the body to wear anything and look fabulous. I had married a gorgeous man. It didn't matter if he wore suits, or jeans, or board shorts.

I was feeling a bit under the weather. We had to finish the photo shoot, but I was vomiting throughout the day. I sent a runner to the pharmacy to get me a pregnancy test. I didn't want to alarm Omar again until I was certain. I thought it might be food poisoning, but I knew what was going on—all this sex we were having.

I waited until we wrapped up the final photo shoot. It was time to confess. I waited until we got on the plane. I leaned over to Omar and kissed him on the cheek.

"What did I do to get such a wonderful peck?"

"Oh, maybe I have some good news for you, baby. I'm … oh, what the hell … we are having a baby!"

He smiled and went to sleep for the rest of the flight.

I got a slight attitude when I got no response from him. A fucking smile? What the hell? I'd expected more. I needed a more than a fucking smile. I eased away from him and rolled my eyes. Talk about a bitch, mad. I waited until the flight landed before I threw a real nigga fit. We got off the plane, and Omar grabbed my arm. "What is your problem, Tracee?"

"Omar, I told you I was pregnant and all you did was smile. I feel like you don't care, so why should I be next to you?"

"I was taking in what you told me. I wanted to fully process that I was getting another bundle of joy from my wife. All you did was react in such an ugly way. Give me a chance to enjoy this. I don't need you to start acting foolish. Let's enjoy the moment."

I paused for a second and then started going off on his ass! "First of all, I felt I responded the way I felt like it. Second, don't tell me how to enjoy my gift to you! Fuck you and your delayed reaction to me, Omar!"

He walked real fast to the car in the parking garage. As I caught up with him, this fool backed up and pulled off, burning nothing but rubber in my face. Such a rage went through my body that I felt I could kill any enemy in plain sight. I was outraged. I couldn't believe this foreign asshole. I loved him, but at the same time I couldn't stand his ass. He'd left me in the damn parking garage with my damn luggage in my hands. This was some bullshit.

I had a moment to think about what the hell just had happened. I'd started to walk toward the double doors when Omar came back speeding around the corner. He jumped out and slapped my tongue down my throat! He was cussing me out in English and Spanish at the same time. I never thought that he would react this way.

"I'm so tired of you and your bullshit, Tracee! I really hate you right now! You are selfish and inconsiderate of my feelings, so bounce, *bitch! Get the fuck away from me!*"

Who in the hell did he think he was talking to? I wasn't no punk as bitch, and I wasn't scared of him. Fuck this shit. I didn't give a damn. It was on and popping right here, right now. I swung on Omar. At this time, the police pulled up. They recognized Omar and questioned him about our dispute. Before he could answer, I yelled to the officer, "Take this man to jail for hitting me!" It was cruel and unusual punishment for me; they obviously didn't see it that way.

The police took my statement. I told them that I was pregnant. Also, I told them that Omar and I had been reacting off of emotions and feelings. I told them that several months ago we had lost our son in a serious car accident. The officers asked us to both calm down and asked if we could settle this at home.

My eye was slightly turning purple—I would have a bruise. I was going to stomp a mud hole in his ass as soon as we got home. Please believe me—it was not over until I said it was over.

The police offered to follow us home. I got into one of the officer's car. We talked the whole way home. I was crying and getting mad just thinking about it all over again. In the back of my mind, I knew I was going to finish what Omar had started.

I'd grown up with male cousins, so I learned to fight hard. I knew this was going to be an all-nighter. I got out and played it off to a tee. I had to make the police think it was all over and done with between the two of us.

Omar and I both watched them pull out the long, curved driveway. I walked toward him and swung with all my might. I hit him like I was fighting a female that I couldn't stand. Blow by blow and hit by hit, I couldn't stop. I had so much anger inside of me. He grabbed me and would not let me go. I screamed and hollered at the top of my lungs. Still, Omar would not let me go. I was out of breath and felt like there was a bear sitting on my chest.

The man must have been out of his rabbit-ass mind to grab me like this. "Omar, you better let me go, 'cause if you don't—oh, my god!" I threatened his ass for a good thirty minutes. He didn't care. He held me until I calmed completely down.

I'd totally forgot that I was pregnant, even though Omar reminded me continuously. Then I reminded him that this was my baby. He called me everything from trash, to stupid, to ignorant, to thoughtless, to inconsiderate. The true question was if I cared what he thought. Ah, no! I sure didn't care. After all, he'd slapped me in front of a crowd. It didn't get any worse than that. This trip had become a disaster. Omar walked into the bedroom and started packing some clothes.

"Tracee, we need some time apart. I need to re-evaluate what just happened. I'm not happy with what I have done to you. Please forgive me, but I must leave."

"Bye, mutha-fucka! Shit, I need to get myself together, too! I think you should leave. This time apart will be good for the both of us."

"Talk to me, baby. Tell me that you forgive me, Tracee."

"I'm not forgiving you for anything, Omar. Just finish packing so you can leave."

I walked into the kitchen as he was packing up some luggage. He walked down stairs with a total of three bags. I watched him leave—he walked out right in front of me. I knew he wanted me to say something to him, but I didn't. I was too stubborn for that.

I called his mother to bring my son home. She said my eye and got upset with Omar. I explained to her what had happened. I also said, "You need to talk with your son. I don't know where he went, and I don't care." I was still mad.

After she brought Junior home, we went to sleep, but I woke up in the middle of night. My entire body was sore from fighting with Omar earlier. I tried not to think about it, but the bruise around my eye was a reminder. I put some frozen peas on it to keep it from swelling, but that didn't work.

When the morning sunshine came through our bedroom windows, I got up and washed my entire body. I was crying so hard and loud that Junior came into the bathroom. I planned a wonderful day with my son.

Melissa called to tell us how great our shoots went. I didn't tell her what had happened, but I did tell her that I'd found out that I was having a baby. She offered to take us out for dinner to celebrate. I told her I wanted to wait until I got a little farther into the pregnancy before celebrating but that later on, we would take her up on the that offer.

This day started off in my favor. There were no interviews that needed to be set up and no photo shoots any time soon. I had time to get my eye together. I called Jerome to get a hair appointment. I asked him to make a house call with the crew. We set a date for the next Friday and called all of my trained professionals, too.

A few days had gone by without any phone calls from Omar. Hell, I didn't call him either. I spent a lot of time indoors. playing with Junior. We both enjoyed our time together. The chef cooked us some remarkable dinners for the next couple of days, although I was throwing up more than I could keep down.

I took a long, hot bubble bath to relax my mind, body and soul. I think my belly enjoyed it more. I went to bed crying—I guess I realized that I had really made Omar mad.

On Friday, Jerome arrived and came strolling right on in, as usual. He looked at me and said without hesitation, *"Bitch, what the fuck happened to you face?"* I looked at him and poked out my lips. "Oh, so now you can't open up yo' mouth to talk? I know you hear me, Tracee. Don't get stupid."

"Whatever, Jerome!"

"You need to be contacting a makeup artist to fix yo' damn face!"

"That's why I called you, the hair expert!" "I can work miracles!"

"I'm a beautician, not a magician!"

"You are such a smart ass!"

"I need to know exactly what happened." As a matter of fact, do you recall that day you came to get your new hair do?" "Before you came in, a female was talking real loud about Omar." "She was bragging about his new house and new contract." "I was just letting her spill her guts out." "Then you came in, and she either figured she was maybe talking a bit much or what, because she stopped talking about him."

"For real, Jerome!"

"Bitch, I was just seconds from going across her head with the curling iron." "You saved her?" Hum, now ain't that something to hear. "Well, I wasn't going to tell you but, maybe now is a good time."

Anything else you are keeping from me? "Well, since you asked, I used to do Omar's girlfriend's sister's hair before I met you." "I stopped doing her hair because I like you!" "I was just taking her money because she had a baller paying for it, and she said to charge whatever I wanted to charge." "I ain't no fool, and I did just what was asked of my services." "Wait, there is a little more confessions I need to make to you."

"Well, as you know, you took Omar from a lot of women. I was always in the mix of most of them. He had enough of them that he ran through. I won't say he tricked his money on them, but he did come up to the shop parking lot quite a lot but not inside of the shop."

"Omar was the ring leader of desperate women searching to find someone to rescue them." "We all know who has the power in this relationship!"

CHAPTER 8

The Basketball Game

M Y DAY WAS COMING TO AN END. ALL OF MY SERVICES were about to be done. I had Jerome wait until I was fully done. I was not done talking to him. I needed some more information. He agreed to wait.

During my massage, Omar had called both the house and my cell phone. "Girl, Omar called, but I didn't answer either of the phones."

"Good! How many times did he call?"

"Six or seven times."

"He will be all right." "He has not called you for ... what? Maybe four days?" "The nerve of him!" "Tacky, are you done yet?" All I could do was laugh. After all, Jerome has a way with words.

As I was getting dressed, Jerome said, "Hey, one of my clients has season passes to all of the Miami Heat basketball games. Do you want to go to a few?""

"My belly is starting to show Jerome, so maybe not."

"Tramp, who in the hell knows that you with child?"

"Just you and my Omar."

"Enough said, T, we going. As a matter of fact I have some tickets for this Sinday."

"Don't you mean this *Sunday*?"

"Look, I said what I said, and I mean what I say—this damn Sinday! Hopefully, you face will be back to normal. Oh, make sure you dress to impress, okay, boo?"

I got my shit in order. Jerome let himself out, and I put on my "please, girl, don't hurt him" outfit. The house phone rang again, and I knew it was Omar. I was upset still, so I didn't answer it.

My hair was looking good. My body was definitely feeling great. I was able to keep food in my stomach. I felt the stress roll away. Omar kept calling, but I kept my composure and did not answer his calls. It was time to get some rest for my big day with my son.

I dedicated my entire Saturday to Junior, and we did everything his little heart desired. I knew he loved the beach, so I packed up a little picnic basket filled with all the goodies and some beach blankets. We packed the Range Rover and drove down to South Beach.

Omar showed up unexpectedly. He must have used the GPS system to track me. He walked right up on me and Junior on the beach, dropped down on his knees, and begged for my forgiveness. "Tracee, I'm so sad, and I have going to bed very unhappy. What do I have to do to come back home?"

"Omar, I need a little more time. I'm not ready to have you back at home just yet."

I allowed him to hang out with us on the beach. Junior was excited to see him. They played and made a sand castle. I was happy to see him, too, but I didn't want him near me.

"Tracee, can we get together tonight to talk? There are some things we need to amend within our relationship. I need a chance to redeem myself about what I did to you and the rest of the family. Please hear me out. I will call you later so we can have dinner and discuss our disagreements."

In the back of mind I told myself, *Whatever, Omar.* I had plans for myself, and he was not going to interrupt them. I told him to call me, even though I wasn't going to answer his calls anyway. I needed to isolate myself some more.

I needed to take my time to heal from everything. I was loving my freedom, even though I was missing him a little bit. We packed up and walked back to the truck. He kissed my belly and spoke Spanish to our unborn child.

He was turning me on. He knew I liked that freaky Spanish shit. It was time to go. I getting too hot in the vaginal area; I wanted him so bad. After all, we did have sex on the beach as often as we could.

I gave him a peck on the check, and Junior gave Omar a high-five. I shed a few tears as I drove into the long driveway. I was hoping he might be right behind me, but he wasn't.

I made pasta with meatballs, and we ate ourselves to sleep. Omar called, but I was too tired to get up to answer. I was worn out from the beach and eating. Omar ended up calling all night long.

Later that night, I rolled over—and Omar was standing right in front of the bed. I screamed, "*What the hell are you doing here?*"

"Tracee, I called you, but you didn't answer my phone calls. I got worried, especially after we talked about meeting up later. I called until I couldn't take it anymore. I needed to make sure my wife and children were okay."

"Well, I was sleeping, Omar. I'm tired. The beach wore us out. I came home and cooked some dinner and then fell asleep.

I would really like you to stay, but if you do, can you sleep in another room?"

"Tracee, I will leave. I'd rather sleep in the same bed with you and enjoy all of you than some of you. Good night! I will clean the kitchen before I leave."

"Thank you!" I rolled over and waited for Omar to walk downstairs.

I had an inner laugh. *This fool is doing whatever to get my full attention.* He was trying his best to stay as long as he could. I knew I was wrong, but I was hurting on the inside. He ended up staying in the house for another hour before he left.

I got up and called Jerome.

"Hello, the beautiful one," he answered. I burst out laughing. It was too late to hear this thang act up. "Tracee, what do you want at this damn hour? It better be good! You are calling me during my catch-up TV sessions."

"Oh, diva, please, I got something that you need to hear."

"Well, damn, can you hurry up and tell me please?"

"I took Junior to the beach today and Omar showed up."

"*What?* How in the hell did he know where you guys were?"

"GPS, bitch!"

"Oh, I will have to get me one of those keeping-track-of-a-mutha-fucka devices. What type of payment do they accept, and where do I get one installed?"

"Ooooo! I should have not called your silly ass. I needed another good laugh."

"Take your tired ass to sleep and just make sure that you are ready for tomorrow's game."

"Good night, Jerome."

"Bye!"

The loud ring of the house phone awakened me. It was Omar. Of course, he wanted to come home. I told him no. I wasn't ready. I knew if he came home that I'd have lost the battle. I wasn't ready to give in. I needed a least a full month, so that he would understand what he could possibly lose. I needed him to repent his sins. I prayed every night for forgiveness. I can't say whether he did or not. I hope he did. Omar had a lot of faith in God. I still needed some healing time.

Jerome came over as Junior and I were eating breakfast. He wanted to see what I planned to wear to the game. "I love these jeans!" he exclaimed when I showed him my outfit. "I have this exact same pair!"

"What?"

"You heard me; I have the same pair."

"You are so silly, diva! I can't wait to go to the game today. I called Momma Velasquez to watch Junior."

After cleaning up and getting ready for the game, I packed Junior's overnight bag. I decided to drive the Bentley. I pulled that bad boy right out of the garage. We dropped off Junior at his grandma's house and bent the corner. We pulled up like true divas. All eyes were on us. Even though Jerome was gay, he was fine. If he hadn't been so flamboyant all the time and a true attention-grabber, he could have passed for a straight man.

Going to the games became a regular routine for us. People started to recognized us immediately—we even had our own fan base at the games. I don't think people really caught on to Jerome's sexuality. We went in VIP style. Jerome pointed out our seats as we strolled down the stairs. When the game started, all kinds of people were shown on the big screens. Jerome pointed out all the undercover gay men in the stands. We had so much fun together—and Miami won the game.

Omar started blowing up my phone; I didn't answer. He called all night, but I was out with Jerome to a nightclub. All of the basketball players were out. They bought me drinks all night long. I didn't drink because I was pregnant, so I passed my drinks to Jerome. At the end of the night, my feet were so sore! I sat down in a corner spot in the club just as Omar walked in.

I was so nervous. I grabbed Jerome and whispered in his ear that Omar had walked into the club with some of his teammates. I was so ready to go. I made it through the crowd, but Omar was right at the door. Oh, my!

"For real, Tracee, for real. So you rather be out in streets than spend time with me?"

"Is this a question, Omar? I ask myself every day if I should be with you!"

"I keep telling myself I need to work things out with you, Tracee." "I'm done!" "I'm so done."

He walked away from me. Jerome ran up and grabbed my arms. "Girl, don't make a scene. Let's go home and think this through, Tracee."

I waited for the valet to pull the car around. We got in and drove back to the house. *The shit hits the fan tonight.* I was mad at Omar for making a scene at the club. He had to make his point.

I sat on the bed and cried. Omar walked in and grabbed my arms. "What is wrong with us?" he asked. "I don't like the way we are acting. I'm moving back home right now. We need to work these problems out."

I asked Jerome to wait for me downstairs while Omar and I had a husband and wife chat. We sat next to each other and held hands. I apologized about everything. I couldn't stop the tears from falling down my face. He was crying heavy tears, too. We needed some time to be alone. I still didn't want him home. I agreed to let him speak his mind. We went back and fourth at least for two hours.

After everything was said and done, I asked him to leave. I felt like the bruise was just the beginning of something worse to happen. I feared him but only when he was angry.

We'd hit each other—that was so unacceptable. The more we discussed our issues, the more I relived my past with Junior's horrible dad. I knew that wasn't a relationship that I wanted to repeat. I had to come up with another way to deal with depression, jealousy, and my exaggerated temper.

Omar would not leave. I walked downstairs to check on Jerome. He was sitting on the couch, all snuggled up in his pink Victoria's Secret robe. "Li'l gal, can you get me some socks so I can go to bed?" I paused to think about it. "Tracee, do you hear me, or am I speaking a foreign language? Walk yo' li'l ass back upstairs with the Grinch who stole Christmas and get me some damn socks! I refuse to be uncomfortable. Get the lead out of yo' ass and handle yo' business!"

"You better be happy that I like you, because I wouldn't allow anyone to talk to me like that, Jerome."

"I don't give a damn. Y'all keeping me up with this bullshit! I'm not about to lose any of my beauty sleep because Ike and Tina can't get along. Can y'all call it a good night so we all can get some sleep? I'm not the nicest person when I don't get my rest."

"Okay, precious, we will chill out. I will end it all tonight."
I went to get Jerome his socks, and then I went to bed.

The next morning Omar woke me up with breakfast in bed.
I guess he thought the fussing and fighting was over. Absolutely
not. I was just beginning. I noticed that I was starting to show a
little more—my belly was poking out.

I'd developed a huge appetite, eating everything in sight.
Even though Omar had cooked, I was still mad. Jerome ran
upstairs to check on me as soon as Omar left. "Good morning,
buttercup! How did you sleep?"

"Great! How did you sleep?"

"Like the beauty queen that I am."

"Well, good, let's go shopping."

"Oh, are we spending your money, or are we spending your
money? Before we go, I need to go home and get my medication
for high blood pressure."

"High blood pressure? Aren't you a little too young to have
high blood pressure?"

"For some odd reason you like me to repeat myself. I said I
got high damn blood pressure. Can you take me home so I can
get my skinny-leg jeans and shoes, please?"

"What about your shirt?"

"The entire outfit."

"Yep! Get your things together, and we can leave." My cell
phone started ringing. Mysterious men were calling my phone
and asking to speak to people that I didn't even know. "Jerome,
did you give my number out?"

"Yes, I did, why are you asking?"

"I'm getting strange phone calls."

"I gave some guys your number instead of my number."

"Wow, thanks a lot. You should have warned me ahead of time."

"Tracee, last night I was so drunk that I gave eight or nine guys your cell number instead of mine. You might be getting some strange phone calls on your phone."

"Oh, so you have jokes! That's not funny."

"You asked me to give you a heads up. I'm following directions."

"Thanks, smart-ass!"

"You're welcome!"

We picked up Junior from his grandma's house. He was happy to see me, but he kept asking for Omar. I had to keep changing the subject.

I needed some maternity clothes. We picked out some of the cutest little shirts and pants. I'm a diva, so I could still walk in pumps. I felt I had a few months before I started really showing. A couple of big shirts to hide my belly would get me through any photo shoot. I only had to worry about my big old belly when it came time to pose in a bathing suit. After all, they do so many photo touch-ups, so this would not be a problem to hide.

I picked out at least eight new outfits. I was ready to get my new look on. "Can we go to Louis Vuitton? I ordered some shoes and a purse for the both of us."

"You bought me something expensive?"

"I sure did."

"Well, then, let's go right on over there!"

"Good afternoon, may I help you with anything?"

"Yes, I ordered two pair of sneakers and a pair of white loafers. Also, I ordered a diaper bag, a denim messenger bag, and a leather tote."

"Can I please have you name, sir?"

"It's Jerome."

"I will take a look and be right back."

"Thanks."

"Jerome, you ordered a lot of items."

"I love Louie. This and Gucci. I can't stay out the stores, either. I can spend a good ten thousand dollars, easily.

"I can, too, especially someone else's ten thousand dollars in U.S. currency."

"Enjoy it, baby girl. You deserve it."

"I can't wait to see everything. Omar will be jealous if I tell him you bought us something."

"I don't give a juicy red fruit about what Omar is going to think. Just as long as you are happy, T—that is all I care about."

"You act like you hate Omar. Every time you get a chance to disrespect him, you do."

"Don't act like you aren't aware of Omar and his little games."

"Sir, I have all but one of your items. Your diaper bag has been shipped. It will be here Tuesday."

"That's fine."

"I will come and pick it up for him."

"We will come back together."

"Your grand total for today is $5,768.24. How would you like to pay for your order?"

"Cash."

I gave Jerome the biggest hug ever. "You're hugging me too tight!" he complained. "I'm going to get wrinkles."

"Whatever!"

"You're welcome. It was the least I could do for you."

"Let's eat some dinner. Pick any place that you want to eat. Dinner is on me."

"Dinner is on your fat belly!"

"Ha, ha, ha! Let's go to eat some Mexican food. I know a great restaurant downtown on South Beach. Let's hurry up. I'm starving. I know Junior is starving, too."

We sat down, and it was really busy inside—so many people inside and outside eating such fine cuisine. We sat right in the middle of everyone. They waiter took our order and brought us some chips and salsa. It was so good.

I turned around to check out the joint and for a second, I thought that I saw Omar in the corner. I got up to take a closer look. As I approached the back of the restaurant, I saw Omar with two of his teammates—and three women.

I stood right where Omar was could see me. He was startled. Jerome ran up quickly to pull me back. "He ain't worth it, girl. He ain't."

"Oh, I can see that by the type of no-class women at the table."

We walked off and grabbed Junior on our way to the truck.

Omar started blowing my phone up. I sent his calls straight to voice mail. I didn't want to hear a thing from him. It was what it was. I saw what I saw. There was no explaining.

I cried the whole way home. I pulled in to and then right back out of the driveway. "Diva, I'm going to stay at a hotel until I figure out what I'm going to do. I need to lie down and rest. I having cramps, and I'm a little disturbed."

"Girl, let's go! I'm glad you bought some clothes. Let's go to Target and get some sanitary items."

"Cool." I turned my phone off. I was done with Omar—officially! I checked myself into a five-star resort.

Omar had wanted to come back home so badly, so I gave him what he wanted. In the back of mind, I wondered why, but after all, maybe this was something that he had been doing all along. He just got caught this time. I knew at that point in time that I was through with him.

After a week I decided to find a condo near the beach. I wanted to be far away from Omar but not too far from my doctor's office. I put a down payment on a three-bedroom, two-bath oceanfront condo. It was guarded, and I paid cash for it.

Omar didn't freeze any of the accounts, so I did what I thought was best for us. I called his mother and told her what had happened.

"Omar is man," she explained, "and that a man will do what he wants to—if you let him."

"I've left him and don't want anything to do with him," I insisted. "Once I get settled, you can pick up Junior if you want to." This would give me a break. I did like my alone time.

The very next day, I bought furniture for the entire home. It was so laid-out. My bedroom was relaxing. Jerome decorated the baby's room with some of the prettiest colors. Junior loved cars and trucks, so his room was so easy to do.

I still was surprised to see that Omar didn't freeze any credit cards or bank accounts. I was always one step ahead of him anyway. I made sure that I paid with cash or a cashier's check. I knew that Omar could track me if I used a credit card.

I was getting bigger. After three more weeks, I couldn't hide my belly anymore. Baby Lourdes was on her merry way. I called

Jerome to see if he wanted to go with me to have my ultrasound to see what the sex of the baby was going to be.

"Hello, the beautiful one. May I help you?"

"Hey, are you going with me or not?"

"Where?"

"The doctor's office, so I can find out what the sex of the baby is going to be."

"Sure."

"I will be ready in a hour."

"I need to get diva-licious."

"Oh, my god. Okay, Jerome, I will see you in an hour."

I got dressed and walked to the elevator. I was walking through the front lobby when Omar walked right up on me. He put his hands on my belly, dropped to his knees, and kissed my belly.

"Tracee, where are you going?"

"Why?"

"I have been looking for you for a month."

"And?"

"I wanted to explain to you who those women were at the table."

"It's in the past, and I want to leave it that way."

"I need to see you and my son."

"You don't have a son."

"Junior is my son, and so is the baby in your stomach."

"Omar, I have to go! I refuse to see you right now."

"I will call you later."

"We will see, Omar. We will see." I was so nervous. He'd caught me off guard. I called Jerome.

"Chello!"

"Hey, Omar was just at my condo."

"*What?*"

"Yes, he was just here trying to explain to me who those women were."

"What did you do?"

"I told him that I had to go. I kept it short and simple. I got the hell right out of there. I am on my way to pick you up!" As I got closer to Jerome's house, Omar started calling my phone again. I didn't answer. I needed to focus on my appointment, not him.

We finally arrived at Dr. Villawow's office and were shown right in for the ultrasound. I was so excited. I wanted to jump for joy. I lay on the table with my stomach burning—I had to pee, but they made me hold it for a better result on the ultrasound.

It's a girl! As a matter of fact, it's twins. I got one of each. Jerome started jumping for joy. I shed tears. I was cursed. Omar had wanted lots of babies.

This is just the beginning of a new beginning, I thought. I made phone calls back home to tell the good news. A few of my girlfriends wanted to start planning my trip back home for a baby shower. I agreed that it would be great to come home in a month and spend some time with my family and friends. I didn't tell them that I had left Omar. I was going to wait until I got back home to spread that news.

Out of respect for Omar, I called him to tell him the news. "Omar, where are you?"

"Driving back to the house."

"Okay, I'm coming to talk to you."

"Okay."

I pulled up and he came right out to open my door.

"Hey, guess what?"

"What?"

"I went to the doctor today. I had an ultrasound. I ... we are having twins." "*Twins?*"

"A boy and a girl."

"I have to call my mother and tell her the good news. I really didn't notice until today that your belly was sticking out."

Well, that really went smooth. Now it was time to tell Omar that I was going back to Vegas to relax for a while. "Omar I need to tell you something else."

"Go ahead."

"I've decided to go back home for a couple of weeks."

"When did you decide this?"

"After our last fight. I'm leaving in a week. I've started packing up some clothes to have shipped."

"What's going to happen to us, Tracee?"

"I don't have an answer for you right now. I hope this time apart will heal both of us."

Omar left very upset. I didn't care. I finally had him in the palms of my hands. There was no turning back. I called Jerome to arrange for him to keep a tight eye on Omar while I was gone. He was too excited to do some undercover work for me.

I called our travel agent to set up a full bedroom suite for Junior and me. I needed a full-service resort. I called to confirm my airline and rental car reservations. Everything was set and ready to go. Omar called. He wanted to spend the rest of the week with us before we left.

I thought that would be great for Junior but irritating for me. I couldn't stand the sight of Omar. My hormones were raging. I felt that at any given moment I would snap. It was time to get the hell away for a while.

Omar wanted to kiss and make up. I definitely wanted to have sex at least one last time. I didn't mind that at all. I set up a hot, sexually seductive night. I had to give him something that he would never forget. After all, I was good at that.

Our days from getting closer. Omar and Junior bonded even more than ever. I enjoyed watching them together. Our night was approaching so fast. I bought candles, body oils, and rose petals.

I ran our bath exactly how he liked it. I bought a sexy little nighty. Everything was coming into play. I asked Omar to take Junior to his mother's to spend his last night with her. While he taking my baby over there, I prepared our long night of hot sweaty sex.

He came back, and I went to the door with nothing on. I walked Omar into the bathroom and started undressing him. He was all smiles. I escorted him into the bathtub, and I climbed in back of him, and he lay in between my legs.

He started crying as I bathed him. I loved the way the water glistened over his body. He was sexy. After our hour-long bath, we started going at it for twenty-five minutes strong. I was on top, then he flipped me over, and he was hitting it from the back. "*Oh, my god! Oh, my god! Oh, my god!*" Those were the only words coming out of both of our mouths. The sex was so good. I felt like I was trying to impress him like we were on our fifth date. He had the best stroke that I had ever felt. He took total control of my precious body; I wanted him to.

It was all night long. I was so tired. I had to do what I had to do. The sun came shining in. We woke up! I took a shower and got dressed. It was time to pick up Junior and head straight to the airport. Omar cried the whole way there.

Fuck his sympathy-crying ass. He wasn't crying when he hit me. I wasn't falling for it at all. I was leaving!

CHAPTER 9

The Shit Hits the Fan

WE SAID OUR GOOD-BYES AND GAVE LOTS OF HUGS AND kisses. Omar was still crying. I gave the best kiss ever. He stopped crying. We walked through the doors and headed for our plane. I didn't look back, because I knew if I did, I would cry. I'm tough. I could handle not crying. I did love him, but I needed time to get my head right. We sat next to a unique woman. She had a story that made me cry. Our conversation was sparked about my son. It went on and on.

Her name was Lauren. She was a real-estate broker in Vancouver, Washington. I asked her about the horrible scar on her neck and that was where it all began. "I was in an abusive relationship for thirteen years with a man named Joseph."

"Why did you wait so long to leave him?"

"I attempted to leave him at least six times. He beat me and locked me in our basement for over three hours every time I tried to leave. I started seeing double images. I started having nightmares of murder. I knew something bad was going to happen."

"What did you do?"

"One night he came home as I was cooking dinner. He threw his plate on the floor and grabbed me by my neck. I tried to pull away from him, but he was a body builder, so of course, he was a lot stronger than me. He started screaming and punching me for no reason at all. I reached for the closest object near me—I grabbed the butcher knife and started swinging at him. He punched me in my stomach and then stabbed me across my neck several times."

"Wow! You're alive to tell this story! I'm amazed by your strength and courage."

"Oh, no, that's just the beginning. After Joseph stopped stabbing me, I turned over and leaped for a knife myself. He was within arm's reach, and I stabbed him in the head."

"*Oh, my god!* You are a strong survivor of abuse. Maybe you should think about writing a book about your love-hate war wounds."

"I might just take you up on that offer, pretty lady. Are you in a bad relationship, too?"

"Actually, I'm taking a big break from one before it escalates into a bad one. Yes, we have had some bad times, and yes, he has hit me, but I also hit him!"

"Are you married to him?"

"Yes."

"Maybe we should take advice from each other and both write a book about it."

"I don't have much to talk about anyway. My life is pretty plain and simple. I'm a model. I'm a personal assistant for my media company. I have been published in several magazines. There is nothing to put in a book about my life."

"You will be surprised what you can come up with on your own."

I was glad to have someone to relate to under these circumstances. Our flight was landing—it hadn't seemed so long this time.

Lauren and I exchanged phone numbers so that we could keep in touch. She went her way, and I went my way. Now it was time for Junior and I to drive to the resort. We checked in and made a few phone calls to let everybody know we had made it safely there. I called Omar, but he didn't answer. I called his mother, and she said that she would contact Omar and let him know we'd arrived.

Oh, well, at least he couldn't say that I hadn't called his Simple Simon ass. By the look on Junior's face, it was time to go. "Let's go see everybody," I said.

"Yeah!" My baby was so excited. My first stop was my mother's home. All of my family was there waiting for us.

As we strolled through the front door, Trinity, Ro-yaltee, Aries, Tiny, and even Pooky jumped out and yelled, "*Surprise!*" I had tears forming in my eyes. To add to my surprise, they'd arranged a beautiful baby shower!

I was speechless. Absolutely speechless. I had so many gifts from everyone. I had the most amazing cake. A bakery had made the cake into a shape of a twin babies. It was so cute. This little getaway was starting off great. It was so good to see everyone. I needed some family love. Being in Miami had changed me. I missed being in Las Vegas.

"So, a little birdie told me that you were thinking about leaving Omar?"

"Who told you that, Aries? How about we all go into the back room and do some catching up?"

"Well, let me tell you something while you're here. I was working at the LGM Grand Hotel and Casino as a fill-in casino waitress one night. I saw Omar there with some of his teammates.

There were women flocking all over him. He excused them away from him. They just kept coming back."

"How do you know it was Omar?"

"He didn't know who I was, but I knew it was him."

"So what happened?"

"Your local whores were working this particular night because it was a Championship Boxing Special Engagement Fight. I watched her humiliate herself in front of him. He grabbed her hand, and they walked away."

"*What?*"

"I didn't want to jump to conclusions, so I followed them. They walked through the casino to the tower suites. I'm not allowed up there during working hours. I waited patiently. I paced back and forth, hoping that I would not miss her walking back from the elevator towers. I did my last round of cocktails, and then I saw them holding hands and walking back through the casino."

"Could you remember how many hours had gone by?"

"At least three or maybe four hours, sweetie."

"Huh!"

"I was trying to figure out the best way to tell you. I didn't want to start any mess. He was still here with a lot of his teammates and maybe she was for one of them."

"Aries, would you believe that story if I told it to you?"

"No."

"I am not convinced at all. I will be calling him about this trip. So this is ho' number one. Is there anything else?"

"Maybe you should talk to Ro-yaltee."

"Why?"

"I think she should tell you."

"Hey, Ro-yaltee, can you come here for a second?"

"Yes, what's up?"

"Tell me your little secret that Aries won't tell."

"Why did you open your big mouth, Aries? It's complicated."

"What's complicated, Ro-yaltee?"

"I'm about to fuck yo' head up with this one. You know how I like porn, right?"

"Right."

"Well, I was at one of my homegirls' houses, kicking it. She was talking about how she had been fucking this ballplayer on and off for six years. She said that they made a sex tape. She was bragging about how big he was and how he could knock the bottom out. I wanted to see who he was. Well, jumping jo-ho-so-fats—it was *Omar*! My mouth dropped. I had to act like I didn't recognize him, so I played it off. I had her stop the tape, and I sparked up a conversation about how and when she met Omar. I also wanted to make sure it was over. She said that he only called her when he coming into town. Also she said that she never kept his number, but she had her same cell number for over ten years and he knew that."

"Are they still messing around, Ro-yaltee?"

"Yes, on occasion."

"This is ho' number two." My whole body went totally paralyzed. I had nothing but evil thoughts running through my mind. I thought for one second that I needed to get my ass on a plane. Nothing could prepare me for my next big disappointment. Last but not least, Ms. Tiny had to add insult to my painful heart.

"Ladies, I need to recap what these women do for a living. Ro-yaltee, what does your hood-rat friend do?"

"Meagan is a bank teller."

"So the bitch can add and subtract numbers. Aries, what does you tramp do for a living?"

"Jewelz is a cocktail waitress at one of the casinos."

"So she's a under cover slut."

"Exactly"!

"Tiny!"

"Girl, I don't know where to start. My story is going to blow them out the water."

"Well, blow the fuck away, then—shit."

"It was a big celebrity basketball tournament about three months ago. I went with some co-workers. On the monitors they started showing a few celebrities on the big screen. I looked up, and it was Omar kissing a woman on the big screen."

"Are you sure?"

"Omar isn't that hard to point out, Tracee. Now this is the icing on the cake. One of my co-workers starting laughing because he knew who the lady was that kissed Omar. While I'm sitting there in shock, he yells, 'My sister is crazy as hell.' 'Yo sister, where?' someone asked him. 'The couple that was just kissing on the big screen,'" I didn't know what the hell to say. "I was hoping that you would see this for yourself. I didn't want to be the bearer of bad news."

"Well, unfortunately, I didn't, Tiny. I'm so mad. I'm frustrated. I'm angry. I married a player for real. Wait ... why were all of you keeping secrets from me?"

"You were happy and no one wanted to hurt you."

"I can understand that. I wouldn't want to tell any of you anything like this either."

"Are you mad at us?"

"Nope! Not at all. I'm going to handle his ass when I get back."

"I got to go to work, so I will catch up with you guys later."

"See you later, Aries! Ladies, I need to lie down for second. I need to process all of this information."

"Come on Trinity, Tiny, and Tracee. Let's go back to the baby shower." It's over, silly girl. "I know, but I at least would like to say bye to everybody. Then say it! "My, you're moody," yelled Tiny.

"Who cares? If you had an in-depth conversation with your supposed-to-be best friends and found out that your spouse is a cheater, then what other fucking mood should I be in, Tiny?"

"I am not the only one who gave you bad news, so take all of your frustration out on someone else."

"Well, fine then, Tiny, have it your way."

"Be nice to her."

"Who do you think you are talking to, Trinity?"

"*You!*"

"Oh, don't think because I'm pregnant that I wont get down on your ass immediately, tramp!"

"Bring it, preggo, bring it. As a matter of fact, I'd like to see you fat ass get off the damn couch and make a move."

"That was cruel."

"You keeping a secret from me was cruel and unusual punishment for me. All of you are about to make me commit a crime. My suspect is Omar. I'm about to be charged with aggravated assault with a deadly weapon. I want him to suffer. I put a lot into this relationship. I have to hold my head up high and act as if everything is okay."

"We are leaving so call us tomorrow, Tracee."

"Okay, Tiny, I will. I'm sorry for what I said to you. I was reacting out of anger, not my heart. I'm not mad at any of you!" There was an empty part in my so-called life. Omar was cheating. I was having thoughts of murder. I wished not to have internal anger. I had to figure out how to make him come clean. He was a man, so I was quite sure he would deny everything. I needed to get some rest. Maybe I would feel better after I got up in the morning.

At that moment, I had strong and powerful pain. I hoped it wasn't a contraction. I hoped this pain was just a big gas bubble. I did just have a full tell-all novel told right in front of me about my husband.

Omar literally was living a secret life. He was something like a pimp. I decided not to call him about the new discovery about his life in Las Vegas. I would keep it on a hush, so that I could check him face-to-face. He apparently did not respect me as his wife. For the next couple of weeks I would focus on having a healthy pregnancy. Then, after the babies were born, I would consider a new life and beginning for all of us.

I decided to spend the night at my mother's. I said all of my good-byes to my guests. It was time to shut it down. I needed my rest. I got into bed, thinking that I could fall asleep with a clear mind. That did not happen. I was angry. My heart was in pain. I needed someone to pray over my body. I needed healing. I decided to go to church tomorrow. *When I'm in God's house, he can hear me! I know he can hear. I feel his spirit present when I'm in his house of worship.*

The next morning, I went to talk to my mom about going to church, but she had already left. I got dressed in a hurry. She had taken Junior with her, which meant I could pace myself to get ready. I went to church early. The parking lot filled quickly. I was so glad that I did go. I needed this. The service started. Pastor Tyrell preached so well that I got the Holy Ghost. This was my first time ever getting the Holy Ghost.

The spirit came over me! I must have had a good experience because I woke up in the lounge area in the back of the church! A sweet little old lady woke me up. Her voice was soothing. "Hey, baby, your in God's hands now. May he rest your soul and give your body strength."

Amen! Amen! Amen! I got up very slowly. I was glad to wake up to a religious woman. She made me rethink all of the mean and cruel things I wanted to do to Omar. I was still mad. I forgave him in my mind, but my heart was still aching.

I didn't know what type of emotions I would experience once I was face-to-face with Omar, but the sooner the better; then I could move on with my life. Church was over, so I decided to call Omar. I needed to hear his voice.

"Hello?"

"Hey, Omar, I was calling to check on you."

"I'm doing fine. I miss baby. I wish we were not fighting."

"Omar once I get back home, we need a real sit-down talk."

"No interruptions, either, baby. I do agree about having the talk."

"How is work?"

"Ah, different, I would say."

"Why?"

"Well, I got a new coach today. I sense some tension between us already. I don't think he likes me."

"Sometimes we might not get along with everybody."

"He can mess up my strategy on the field and put someone else in my spot."

"That will not happen. You took the team to three World Series. They would be a fool to remove you from your leading spot."

"It's all politics. When are you coming home?"

In the back of my mind I had already said I wasn't going to be honest. I wanted to catch him off guard. "In two weeks, baby!" I was rolling my eyes the entire time that I was talking to him. He disgusted me. I couldn't see Omar doing all of those dirty things. I honestly could not wait to see his expression when I came home. He was going to get busted. Operation Totally Busted and Disgusted in full effect. I wrapped up the conversation with "Omar, *I love you!*"

"*I love you, too, baby!*"

If only he meant what he'd said. I wasn't giving Omar any more chances. He was not ready for me. I had something for that ass.

I was getting teary-eyed. I wanted to cuss him out. I did love him, but I hated him, too! These mixed emotions were killing me. I drove back to the hotel to take a long hot bath. I soaked in the tub and passed out. I was asleep for two hours before the phone woke me up. I was startled. "Hello! Who is this?" I could hear breathing on the other end of the phone. I took the phone away from my ear and looked at the caller ID to see who was calling me. That damn Jerome!

"Hey, boo, hey! When are you going to be done soaking your royal oaths?"

"How do you know that I am soaking—or better yet, did soak—my royal oaths?"

"I know you like the back of my hand."

"I think we just were spending too much time together."

"Ooooo, don't like that with your grumpy self."

"So what are you doing, Jerome?"

"Hair and some makeup."

"Oh, where are you going?"

"To Popeye's."

"Popeye's?"

"Yeah, there is something new for me working the register, girl."

"Wow!"

"Okay, I do need to talk to you about something very important."

"What?"

"If I died, would you cry?"

"What kind of question is that?"

"I'm asking you for a reason."

"Of course I would. You shouldn't even ask me about a thing like that. I love you like the sister that I never had."

"You're the sister I always wanted."

"Thanks!"

"If you had to give a speech about me, would you?"

"Yes! Yes! Yes! Jerome stop stalling and ask the question."

"I have one more question to ask you, Tracee."

"I'm ready."

"I have lived my life in sin. I have tried to make things right in my life. I have asked for forgiveness. I have asked God to show me the righteous way to live my life. I have slept with so many men in life unprotected. I am afraid of death. I was at work last week when I got a phone call from my missing-in-action uncle in Cuba. Well, as you are aware, my dad was an immigrant from Cuba."

"Okay."

"The money he made, he sent back to his mother. I didn't know my family members there at all. My so-called father died. My uncle Xavier, who is his only brother, called to tell the news. I asked how he found me, and he said they always knew where I was. I asked him why he was contacting me now, and he said my mother told them not to contact me. I asked why, and he said because my dad used to beat her, and they made arrangements for me to never meet or see him. I'd asked when I was young how we lived so well, and she said my father was dead and that he left us a lot of money. I believed her. It was all a lie. My uncle said, out of respect and the fact that my dad was on drugs real bad, that he agreed to the terms with my mother."

"How did your dad die, Jerome?"

"Damn, I'm trying to tell you everything, heffa. Anyway, he died from cancer."

"*Cancer!*"

"Oh, that's not the icing on the cake, boo-boo. This man was filthy rich. I was his only child, and he left everything to me."

"So are you rich, or are you wealthy?"

"I'm both! I was calling you to help me get my flights together and to ask you if you could go with me."

"Jerome, I'm really hurting from the bad news about Omar and his trips to Vegas. As a true friend, I need time to think, but as your supporter, I will be there for you!"

"Tracee, maybe you need to go and clear your mind. I'm going to go see what he looks like and to talk and sign paperwork. I figured because you were all into legal matters, that I would have your expertise in this matter."

"Fool, now you know I'm not an attorney."

"I know. I just wanted you to be there with me. I need you here with me."

"I'll come back tomorrow. When do you need to get to Cuba?"

"My uncle said that they are going to bury him in Miami. The funeral is in two days."

"I'll leave from here late tomorrow, and I'll call you as soon as I get into town."

"I will have to meet all of my Cuban family members and since you are my closest friend, I wanted you with me."

"No problem." I hung up with Jerome and started packing. I wasn't calling Omar to tell him that I was coming into town. I cut my trip short. Jerome was there for me, and I needed to be there for him. I went to see my mom. My old classmate had come by to see me. When I first walked into the house, I didn't realize who he was.

"Hey, Tatum, how are you?"

"I had to come by and see your mom. I saw a magazine with you on the cover. To my surprise, your mom was still living in the same home. How are you?"

"Good! I live in Miami with my husband and son. I'm having, as you can see, another bundle of joy."

"We should exchange e-mail addresses because I'm always in and out of Miami on business."

"Wow, for real!"

"Yeah!"

"All right, we can." So I did just that. I gave him my e-mail, and kissed my mom, and left to go finish my rounds. I was gone all day long. I didn't care. I needed to see everyone before I left. My phone rang, and it was Jerome again.

"Hey, I got some more news about my dad. He invested in some stock and the market shot through the roof during the time of his investing. I was listed as next of kin. They wanted to set up a meeting with me after the funeral."

"Then set the shit up! I hope your dad hooked you up! I think this is great for you after all of the horrible experiences with your bad money decisions. Maybe this is your time to shine. This is a wake-up call, Jerome. I know as your friend that you will take into consideration what is about to happen to you! You are a celebrity, anyway. Money, power, and respect are the least of my worries. All I ask is that you don't have a relapse, but if you do, please feel free to contact me for help."

"Damn, Tracee, I will not follow down that yellow brick road again! It was so hard to recover from the addiction. You are my positive influence. I will always take care of you and family. I appreciate our friendship, and I don't trust anyone but you."

"That makes me feel special."

"Oh, special, bitch!"

The funeral had come and gone. Jerome looked his best as usual. I didn't get much sleep. Jerome kept me up the night before, prepping himself. After the burial we had to meet the attorney at his office to discuss financial possibilities.

"Hello, my name is Jaden Alexander Mohavier. I'm your father's attorney. I have known him for twenty-five years now. When I heard that he had passed, I was upset that he did not tell me he had cancer. Your father lived his life to the fullest. He also stated that he and your mother had set up a verbal agreement between them. I thought it was stupid then, but he always knew your whereabouts. I had a private investigator locate your place of employment. This is why we are here today."

"This is my friend, Tracee. I would like her to be in the room during this meeting."

"Sure."

"I not sure, Jerome, if you are aware of the type of money, stock, and commercial property that your had."

"No, sir, I'm not."

"When you were a child, your father set up a trust. In the trust until he died was when you would have full rights to all of this."

"Who me?"

"Yes, I have been watching your investments grow."

"How much do have?"

"Well, as of right now, five million dollars in cash, seventeen million dollars in stocks and commercial property, meaning the land owned by you is twenty million."

"I'm worth forty-two million dollars?"

"Actually, Jerome, you're worth an estimated sixty-four million dollars."

"God bless America. Where is my check?"

"We actually have to configure how you want your money distributed out. If you continue to invest like your father did, you will never have to work again."

"*Wow!*"

"You have to appoint a beneficiary of your estate."

"I will appoint Tracee Velasquez, my best friend."

"Jerome, please don't do that!"

"Tracee, I have shared a lot of sob stories, and you have always been there for me. I want to return something greater back to you."

"I accept!"

"Mr. Mohavier, could we do the paperwork now, before Tracee changes her mind?"

"Yes. All I have to do is add Tracee on, and that is that. Tracee, can you sign on all of the dotted lines? Also, Jerome, I need you to give to me a bank account number so I can set up a wire into your account every month for twenty-five thousand dollars."

"Here is my check with my account number, Mr. Mohavier."

"Give me a few minutes and everything will be set up for you."

"Okay!"

"Also, you will have complete access to two million in cash."

"In cash?"

"Yes, sir. Everything is confirmed now, and you will get a wire for twenty-five thousand dollars in less than an hour."

"Tracee, when we leave there is an issue we need to discuss. I have been talking to my doctor, and there is no other way to say this to you. I want to tell you about an important event that will take place. I've decided to get a body transformation."

"*What?* Did I hear you correctly?"

"Yes."

"Jerome, what do you mean a body transformation?"

"I want to have a sex change! A sex-mutha-fuckin-change, bitch! I want to change into the woman that I'm supposed to be."

"Jerome, there is nothing wrong with you. I know you think there is, but you are so perfect. Even if you change your body parts, it won't make you a woman."

"Bitch, all I need to feel complete is a woman's body parts."

"Jerome, please think this through. I don't need you trying a new trend just because you have money. You need to invest and take care of yourself for the rest of your life."

"I will think about it longer, but I have been wanting to do this for a long time."

"My biggest issue with you wanting to have a sex change is that you might not like yourself afterward. This is not something you rush into. Please wait a couple of months before you make your final decision."

"I will. After all, you are my best friend forever."

"Jerome, also I hope you are doing this for yourself and not for another man fantasy. You know my motto is always 'Do you; don't do me.'"

"Tracee, don't start today. We are having such a good time, so let's end it with a good evening. I have a list that I put together, and I expect you to help me with it. I'm leaving it with you, and I want your opinion, if you can help. Also, drop me off at the shop so I can pick up some supplies before you take me home."

"Yes, Miss Daisy! Anything else?"

"That will be it."

I kept quiet during our short drive back to the shop. I was trying to process this whole body-changing experience that Jerome was trying to go through. I really didn't want him to do it. I felt he was gorgeous. I told him when I first met him that he was too damn pretty. I felt he was going to make the biggest mistake of his life. He would regret it. As his friend, all I could do was voice my opinion and hope he listened to me. My worst fear was Jerome going to the extreme—and extreme he is. I dropped Jerome off and went straight home. To my surprise, El Stupido was waiting for me.

"Hi, Omar! How long have you been waiting for us?"

"Oh, about thirty minutes. I was so happy that you came back. Tracee I miss you so much. Life has been hectic without you. I was waiting for you to get back to have a real talk. I don't know where to start because a lot has changed for me."

"Follow me up to my new house so we can talk."

"I want to confess everything to you."

"Start talking. I will not say that I can accept this from you, but I will hear you out!"

"Tracee, I have been cheating on you since we very first started dating. I have been with many woman. At the end of the day, I felt like shit every time I lay down with these whores. They meant nothing to me. I thought this was a life that I wanted. In return, I lost you and my unborn baby. I don't expect you to forgive. I just would like to be around you. It's odd that even though I have cheated on you more than once, I still was crazy in love with you. I can't see you with another man, but I know there will come a time for me to see you with someone else. I want to apologize to you. I'm so sorry, and I never meant to hurt you. I enrolled myself in a Sex Addicts Anonymous class. I'm sick, Tracee. I needed help. I got help. When you left, I had a lot of time, and this is how I spend my spare time."

"Now it's time for me to talk to you, Omar. Let's put Junior to bed. Omar, I had a small taste of what it would feel like, not having you around. The very first fight we had, I had developed a slight case of anorexia. I didn't like that. I slowly started to feel depressed. I knew you were cheating, and I allowed it. I should have addressed it sooner, but I didn't. I tolerated everything you did. I knew women were calling you, and I still denied it to myself. I have phone records, hotel receipts, room keys, etc. Anything you may have felt that I did not have or know, I did. I knew about your so-called secret meetings every other week. I even know where this bitch lives. I'm not too stupid. I'm very bright. I followed you more than once. I was preparing myself to leave you. I just wanted it to be the right time. I'm looking forward now and yes, you will be a part of our baby's life.

"As far as us, there is no more us. I want to live my life without being married. You feel and act like you're single. I will always love you, but I will not love a man as hard as I loved you. It is a total shocker to me that even though you knew my past that you didn't change. You had me move out here, promising me a better life. All I got in return was another baby, some money, a best friend, a new home, some money, a new career, some more money, a couple of vehicles. Damn, what else could a girl ask for? In return to you, Omar, I would like to say thank you for being you, and thank you for showing me how to make the best of what you have and go for what you want.

I want a divorce immediately! I want you to leave my house. I hope you find a great attorney. If you care when this is all said and done, Omar, just make the divorce easy on yourself. It will

159

be easy for me. I have some things I need to attend to, so could you please leave?"

Omar had a shocked look. I meant everything I said. I wanted to read this list that Jerome had left in my bag. Omar sat with his eyes all red from crying, and I walked toward my room. "Omar, when you are done crying, lock my damn door before you leave. *Good night!*"

I lay across my big bed and read Jerome's list. As usual, he was being a total diva. He wrote everything he ever wanted and needed on a list, numbered perfectly from one to thirteen:

Jerome's What I Want List

1. Full sex-change operation
2. New wardrobe
3. Five-bedroom, three-and-a-half bathroom house with a three-car garage
4. Black Range Rover
5. 750 LI BMW (cocaine white)
6. 1950 Cadillac (pink)
7. Black convertible Bentley (two-door)
8. My own beauty salon
9. My own clothing line (B-Black)
10. Yacht
11. Eight-carat a piece diamond earrings
12. Thirty-five carat bracelet
13. Twenty-five carat watch

I laughed myself to sleep. That damn Jerome was too funny. The silly part was that he would buy all of those items in a day if he could. I knew he would. As I got farther into the list, I heard Omar leave. *Thank you.* I was hoping he was not going to stay. My belly was tight, and he was the reason for it. I was not going to get any sleep with him in the house. If I'd been in my right mind, I would have gotten some of that before he left. Oh well, I would take care of that soon. I grabbed my phone to tell Jerome about my encounter with Omar. He didn't pick up. I called him several times and left urgent messages. He still didn't call me back. I tried to stay up, but I passed out.

CHAPTER 10

Rebirth of a Real-Ass Woman

WOKE UP THE NEXT MORNING TO JEROME'S RING TONE. I HAD eight missed calls from Omar as well. I called Omar back to see what he wanted. The phone rang until his voice mail picked up. I had to leave a message.

I called Jerome to see if he wanted to get his items on the list started. "Hey, I'm on my way to get you, so be ready."

"Tracee, don't be calling me early in the damn morning."

"I packed up my out-all-day bags and put on a simple yet cute outfit. I called my mother-in-law to watch Junior. As I was walking out the door, my house phone rang.

"Babe, I was wondering if we could meet tonight."

"Why, Omar?"

"I need to be around you and Junior. So can I come by tonight?"

"I guess. Omar, I guess."

"I'm going to call you later."

"*All right!*" I got into my truck and drove to Omar's mother's house. I gave my baby a hug and walked him into his grandma's house. "I'll be back to get Junior later, and thanks!" I sped off. I connected my Bluetooth so I could call Jerome. "Sexy, I'm outside."

"If you would have taken any longer, I could have had V-8!"

"What the hell ever, Jerome!"

"I'm just saying, I could have."

"Let's go to the Bentley dealership first. I made an appointment with my realtor, Nina Smith, so we could look at the pictured listed houses for immediate move-in."

"What time?"

"We have a 3:30 appointment."

We pulled up to the dealership, and every gay man that day had to be working. Jerome was having a field day, making them work for his sale. "Excuse me, can I test-drive this convertible right here?"

"Yes, you may, sir."

Jerome was out of control! I was having fun watching him in action. When it came down to the price, he turned into a *Deal or No Deal* contestant. After several hours of flirting and eyelash-batting, the salesmen gave into Jerome's price. Thank heavens, because they were all working my nerves. Before we left the dealership, he asked them to deliver the car on a flatbed tow truck with a big-ass pink bow around it! *Wow!* All I could say was *wow!*

"Ah, Jerome, where are they delivering your car?"

"To your new house, bitch. I need a safe place to park it until I get my own place. I thought you knew. If you didn't know, now you know my plans."

"Jerome, you are out of your rabbit-ass mind. I only have two parking spots, and I do have vehicles of my own."

"Well, you need to make room for one mo'! Where do I sign?"

"For real, Jerome, for real. I have no say in this pick-up-and-delivery discussion?"

"No. not to my recollection. Let's go! Thank you, sir, and could you please call before you deliver the car?"

"I sure will."

"Jerome, we still have time to get at least two or more items on the list before we go see Nina Smith, the realtor."

"Okay, let's go shopping."

"Great!"

"I can't wait to go and spend some money on new clothes and jewelry. Nothing but the finest for me. I want to go to Gucci, Prada, Louis Vuitton, D&G for men, Lacoste, Ed Hardy vintage store, and last but not the least, Niketown."

"Your wish is my command."

We shopped for hours. We made so many trips to drop off bags into the truck that we ran out of room. It really didn't matter because Jerome had time to go to the diamond wholesale district to buy loose diamonds. He bought at least thirty loose diamonds.

"How much did you end up spending, Jerome?"

"For the diamonds, it was $200,000 for flawless round cuts."

"I meant the total, fool!"

"Nunyah."

"What?"

"I said nunyah."

"Quit playing with me, Jerome, and answer the question.

"In Gucci I spent $7000; in Louis Vuitton, $17,000[in D&G for men I spent $2500; and in Lacoste, $3500; Ed Hardy, $4000; and of course Niketown—shit, the new J's alone ran me a good $3000. I spent a total of $437,000!"

"Oh, don't let me forget some skinny jeans!"

"For who?"

"Me!"

"Ah, don't you mean big-girl jeans, because you are pregnant?"

"Everything is a joke, huh, Jerome?"

"Yeah, like you could actually fit in those jeans."

"I'm going to get me some, too!"

"Hurry, so we can get to our next adventure of the day!"

"Not too bad! All that in just a matter of three hours. Good job! Let's go see some houses."

"Yeah!"

We arrived at the sales office of my realtor. She was happy to see that we showed up on time. As you know, black people are never on time for anything.

"Welcome. Come on in and have a seat, please."

"What type of houses do you have to look at right now?"

"Well, I have a couple of four-bedroom houses and five-bedroom houses on the beach. Which would you like to see first?"

"Jerome. she is talking to you, not me."

"Oh, let's go see the beach properties first."

"Let me grab my keys, and we can ride in my sales truck."

Cool! We looked at so many properties along the beach. Jerome fell in love with a mansion so laid-out. It was a bit pricey, but nothing was too pricey for the new millionaire.

"Ms. Nina, I want this house. Boo, I don't need to look at any more homes."

"Sweetie, we need to look at least three more houses to narrow down what you want."

"This last house we looked at had everything I want in a home. Let's negotiate a price."

"Well, they asking for a high four million."

"I'm only going to pay a high two million. Tell them to take it or leave it. Also let them know the funds can be wired into their account with twenty-four hours."

"I will call the owners now, and we can make a deal."

"Do that, honey, so I can furnish this home."

"Jerome, give me an hour to talk with them. Why don't you and Tracee go and eat and then come back! I have one more question for you Jerome."

"Sure."

"Are you set on paying between 2.5 and 3 million?"

"I'm not paying more than 2.8 for the house, in cash."

"That's all I needed to know. I'll call you guys in an hour."

"Tootles! Come on, Tracee, with your wobbling fat ass! I want to go the boat dealership."

"We don't have time!"

"I only want to look, okay, precious?"

"*Whatever!*"

We drove about fifteen minutes away from the sales office to a boat dealership.

"This is a nice boat. I like this one, Jerome."

"I don't care which one you like."

"It is nice, though."

"You already acting funny style with you money. Catch on, boo, catch on!"

"Excuse me, sir. What is the price tag on this fifty-four-foot yacht?

"Twelve million."

"Damn! I'm going to wait on that."

"Good! I told you this was a waste of time."

"Tracee, I'm dying."

"*What?*"

"I said I'm dying, and it's internal. The doctors said that they don't what is wrong with me and they can't figure out why I'm bleeding internally. I have been to several doctors, and my next visit will be to an herbalist. I don't know where else to turn. I'm scared and mad at the same time."

"Jerome, you are a diva, and you will be fine. I trust you pray every day. You need to pray for forgiveness first, and repent your sins and ask God to guide you."

"I pray for a lot of things, but I pray for you more."

"Me?"

"Girl, I have to make sure you survive the sitcom reality show of *The Real Housewife of Omar Velasquez!*"

"Yeah, I thought you knew."

"I bet if we recorded y'all on a daily basis, we could get some serious money and endorsements. He is a popular man and everybody loves to see him."

"Oh, please, Jerome! I will not be starring, co-writing, or co-producing any more damn drama series. I also will not give America a new reality TV show! I'm happy modeling and being a mother. Anyway, back to you! I'm going to pray harder and more for you! I need you around. Who will watch my baby, love my babies, and teach them how to run the show completely?"

"America, it is me! I will take HYB for $600, Alex!"

"You are so crazy! I need you, and you need me. We have a bond like no other."

"I'm no angel, Tracee, but I do want your full support. These last days have been so good for me. I'm living every day to the fullest now. I don't know when my last day will be here, and I want every day to be lived to the fullest. I'm so happy right now. My phone is ringing, so hold up a second. Hello? Hey, yes, we are coming back to your office right now. I hope they approved my offer on the house."

"Let's go and find out."

"Hold my hand; I'm so nervous."

"Drama queen."

"Okay, I talked to the owners of the home, and I made an offer they couldn't refuse."

"So how much?"

"They took the two million cash offer.

"Oh, my god! I'm so happy for you."

"Where do I sign?"

"It's going to take me about thirty minutes to print the papers, and you can sign them today. I'll fax over the documents for the owners to sign, and we can close escrow in a week."

"A week? Why?"

"You need to get a home inspector in immediately. Then you will need to have the funds wired to the title company."

"Wow, you make it sound so simple."

"As long as you are not financing, it is that simple."

"Cool."

"I'll call you in week to come back and sign the title and escrow documents."

"Thank you so much, Nina."

"My pleasure! Thank you, Tracee, for introducing me to Jerome."

"You're welcome. Let's go and have a celebration dinner."

"Miss Thang, I thought you had a date with Omar tonight."

"I knew you were a comedian, Jerome. Why are you laughing?"

"I'm just saying I thought you and Omar had some unfinished business."

"Jerome, do you want to go or not?"

"I need to go home and change."

"Okay, so I'll take you home to grab your things, and we can party like a rock star tonight. We have a lot to celebrate!"

"My house, my car, my new wardrobe, my money."

"Let's party like the rock stars that we are. Go and get you stuff and come right back."

"I'll call Omar and have him come to watch Junior while we go and hang out."

"You are so wrong for that. You are fully aware of Omar wanting to be in your presence; that he will do anything for you!"

"I'm just using all of my resources."

"Resources, my ass."

"I ain't mad at you."

"I'm learning."

"I'll call him when we pick up Junior from Grandma's house. I'm starting to feel a little sick, but a little ginger ale can fix that.

"I'm starting to feel like a shot of Patrón would make me feel better too."

"You are a hot mess. Come on, let's get ready to have some fun!"

"How are you going to have fun with a big stomach?"

"I'm going to look sexy tonight!"

"Skinny jeans on pregnant bitches are not cute. Please wear some maternity clothes tonight. I don't want to get motion sickness."

"Motion sickness?"

"Yeah, when you walk, I seem to feel like I'm on a ship, and it is rocking back and forth. You are not going to give me a headache tonight! You are not going to make me seasick tonight."

"Leave me alone and go get ready! I'm going to call Omar."

"He is going to want some of your fresh-baked cookies tonight."

"Shut up!"

"Cookies, cookies, cookies!"

"I forgot the reason why I'm your friend."

"I'm the only reason why you get up every day and smile."

"You can sell the bullshit to someone else."

"Whatever! I'm going to relax in bath while you have phone sex with Omar."

"Cut it out! I'm going to get him over here so we can leave."

"Roses are red and violets are blue. Omar is a cheater, and he slept with whores, too!"

"No comment. I'm calling him, so go and get ready. Omar, can you come and watch Junior while I go hang out with Jerome for a few hours?"

"I'm on my way!"

"Jerome! Jerome, he didn't give me the third degree about hanging with you."

"I'm bathing. I'm in timeout mode."

"Can you go soak it and scrub it?"

"I'll talk to you when I get out."

"I'm going right now."

I put out several different outfits to wear. I decided to let Jerome pick my outfit. My mood changed, so I really didn't want to put on clothes. Jerome went all out on his outfit. He was fashion statement waiting to happen.

"So what is the beached whale wearing tonight?"

"I was hoping you could pick it."

"Wobble to the side so I can see what you have laid out to wear. Oh, this is so naked and so not pregnant. This is your ready-to-wear, going-out-with-Jerome outfit."

"I'm pregnant, not crazy.

"This is a new-you outfit. Like it, wear it, work it."

"Okay! I'll get real sexy only for you.

"I'm doing your hair and makeup."

"That's fine!"

"You will be the envy of all pregnant women."

"I hope!"

"Omar will hate on you."

"That is my true intention. Alrighty, as soon as dumb-and-dumber gets here we can leave. I spoke too soon. He is here, and I'm too damn sexy."

"Yeah, momma, this is the Tracee I know."

"I'll get the door while your appearance."

"Hey, Omar."

"What's up? Tracee, where are you?"

"I'm coming!" As I walked into the room, his eyes lit up like firecrackers. I knew I was too sexy and a tad bit naked to be pregnant. "Let's go! Thanks, Omar, I'll see you a little bit later."

"Y'all have fun, and keep my wife safe, Jerome."

"I will, Omar."

We ate and danced the night away! I had the time of my life. I could tell Jerome was enjoying himself. He was drunk as hell. It was time to call it quits. He drove back to my house. Jerome started crying. "Tracee, you are my best friend and no matter what, I will always be there for you and your family."

"I know, diva, I know."

"I hate Omar for making you unhappy. I have never gotten up enough strength to tell him that he messed up a good thing."

"Sweetie, he is aware of what the hell he was doing all along. I'm not putting up with him or his bull anymore. I'm not mad; it's more of a relief for my unborn child and me. I'll deal with him on my time, my turf, and my way. I'm not going backward. I'm moving forward."

We arrived back home; Jerome was fast asleep. Omar and Junior were up eating ice cream. Of course, he wanted to talk. I listened to Omar pour his heart out. I didn't care about his feelings. I told him how I felt. I reminded him of all the woman and lies. "I can't be with you, Omar. We can be here for the children, but after the baby is born, I'm moving back to Vegas."

"No, you're not, Tracee. I'll fight you in court for my baby, Tracee. I will."

"Omar, I don't care! Do what you have to do, Omar!"

"I didn't come here to fight with you. I came to rub your belly and spend time with the both of you."

"So do it then, Omar! Be a man for once. Be here for me and not for you! I put up with so much of your mess, Omar."

"Tracee, please just stop. You're getting upset, and I want to lie next to you. I want to be here. I know I messed up bad, but I need you, babe! I do! I will do whatever it takes to make it right between us."

"There is nothing you can do to change all of the mistakes you have already made. I want us to be here for our kids, and that's it. I don't care about the past anymore. Omar, I just want to live drama-free. You, Omar, are the cause of the main drama issues in my life. All of the women, the lies—it is time to put it in my past. I'm ready to move on."

"Hello, I know this is your house, Tracee, but can you be quiet? I need all of my beauty sleep. What do I have to do to get some damn quiet around here? I'm not the nicest person with less than eight hours of sleep."

"Good night Jerome. I will try to keep it down."

"A bitch needs her rest."

"Tracee, I don't know how you put up with him and his ways."

"Omar, at least he is always truthful with me. I'm going to bed, Omar. Good night!" I waited an hour before I went into my baby's room to get some real sleep. I didn't care if Omar felt alone. This was my house!

A whole new day arrived, and Jerome made plans for a new body transformation. "Tracee, I just talked with the plastic surgeon, and I'm going in for a consultation. I'm so excited. The new me is on the way."

"I can't believe you are really going through with this sex-change operation."

"I will, and I am."

"Well, it is what it is! I'll support whatever you are doing."

"Good."

"When are you going?"

"I'm glad you asked. I get the keys to my house today, and I'm going for my consultation tomorrow. I will pull up in my new Bentley."

"I'm going to relax today and absorb last night—and now, your newly entered information. I need time to process this. I'm being supportive for all of your needs. You have been there for me with all of the Omar drama series."

Jerome left. Omar shortly followed. I had peace of mind at last. I needed some alone time. *I'm going to take a long, hot bubble bath. This will relax me. Junior is a good boy, and all I ever wanted was a father for him. I feel like my life is coming together, even though soon there will be no more Omar. I have a career to think about. I have a new image. I'm going to be Mommy and Daddy. My kids will need me. I'm leaving Miami, and I need to tell Jerome and Omar that my mind is made up!*

I woke up—my water bag broke! I was rushed to the hospital. A nurse called Omar and Jerome to come to ER. I was in so much pain, and I was worried about Junior's being with a complete stranger. I prayed for Omar to get there fast. He did. I was happy to see him but mad at the same time. He kissed my forehead. I smiled but on the inside, I couldn't stand him. The doctor came in and started laying out his tools for delivery. I was on an IV with medication to help with the contractions. I could feel the baby drop lower.

Jerome entered the room. "I thought a saw a potty tat."

"What?"

"I said, I thought I saw a potty tat."

"Are you talking about my va-jay-jay?"

"Yes! Why do you have all out for everybody to see?"

"I don't; the doctor is getting ready for me to push the baby out."

"*Wow.*" All of sudden, Jerome passed out on the floor. At first I thought he was being dramatic. He didn't move. I pushed the call button and screamed for the nurse to come in. A whole bunch of nurses ran in. They took him out right away.

I was crying, and the nurses were trying to keep me calm. I was in labor so every emotion was running through my body. I was scared. I kept asking questions, and no one would give me a straight answer about Jerome.

My doctor walked back in and told me it was time to start pushing. I did, and I did. I pushed three times, and my baby boy came out. I was like, "Look—a little Omar." I thought I was having a girl, even if it was a boy. I was happy. I called my nurse because I was worried about Jerome. I closed my eyes and said a little prayer for Jerome. I opened my eyes, and Omar was holding our son.

"Tracee, please, baby, don't leave me. I promise I will do better and right by you."

"Omar, this is not the right time to talk about our relationship. Can you go and find out what is going on with Jerome?"

"Yes, I will." Omar walked out. I was in so much pain. I wanted to know what was going on with Jerome. Omar walked back in with this messed-up look on his face. "Tracee, it doesn't look good for Jerome. The nurse said Jerome has full-blown AIDS, and he was living his last days."

"I wasn't aware of any sickness that he had. Where is Jerome?"

"They took him to ICU. He is unconscious."

"Unconscious! Oh, my goodness!"

"The doctor said he would not make it."

I started crying. I couldn't believe he'd done this to me—all this time he was sick and hadn't told me. I couldn't believe it. I was sad and mad at the same time.

Omar was very comforting to me. I wanted to see my friend, but they made me stay in bed. I asked for his nurse's station information to keep in contact with them until he woke up.

"Baby, they said he's not going to wake up."

God, please don't take my friend without me saying my good-byes to him. Please let my friend open his eyes to see my baby boy. I need him in my life. I need him to wake up! I fell asleep. I woke up in the middle of the night to a voice talking to me. Jerome was talking to me! He told that he was fine, and it was time to leave this earth. I was scared and happy to hear him. I told him to hold on until they released me to come see him. I thought I was up, but I was in a deep dream. When I did wake up, I was still in the hospital bed, and Omar was on the couch. My baby was in his hospital bed, sleeping. I asked to wash my body while my Omar was still in the room. I cried in the shower about Jerome. I could cuss him out, but that wouldn't justify anything. He was here, and it was what it was.

I got myself ready for our departure. I was happy to give birth, but I wanted to see Jerome. Omar drove us home. I asked him to stay at my house while I went to see Jerome in the hospital. He agreed to stay.

I changed my clothes and even though I was in so much pain, it didn't matter. I needed to see Jerome. I arrived at the hospice.

They made me cover up my entire body with a protective gown. I also had to wear a mask. I entered the room only to see a room full of strangers.

"Harpo, who dees people?"

I laughed! Jerome was feeling better.

"What took you so long? I could have had a V-8."

"Maybe you should have had one for the both of us."

"Where is the ugee baby, anyway?"

"Omar has him."

"What?"

"That's right. Omar has little Omar and Junior."

"I know you are not happy with the way Omar has been behaving, but I hope you will find it in your heart to let it go."

"I can't believe you are asking me to forgive him after all the drama he put me through."

"The point is, he is trying to change, and change is good."

"Whatever! So, you have been sick. When were you going to tell me?"

"I wanted to live my last days the way I wanted to. I'm happy, and I really wanted to see little Omar."

"Well, you have to get better, and I'll bring him and Junior to see you." I leaned over to kiss Jerome—and all of a sudden, he flat-lined.

All the doctors came running in. I was escorted out of the room. I ran out to the front of the hospice waiting room to call Omar. I screaming and yelling to tell him what had happened. As Omar was trying to calm me down, Jerome's doctor came out to get me. "Omar, I will call you back!"

"Hello, my name is Dr. MacDowden, and I'm Jerome's head doctor. Here are some papers you will need to fill out."

"Papers! Fill out! What are you talking about?"

"Jerome has you down as his next of kin, and he didn't make it. We were unable to save him. In order to make arrangements for his burial, you have to sign all of these papers. Did he have a will?"

"As a matter of fact, he did, and I will call his attorney right now." I did just that. I got on the phone and talked with Jerome's attorney. He knew I was not in my right mind. I needed a time-out for myself. I needed to pull myself together. I sat down and cried until my eyes were bloodshot. I went back inside to see Jerome for the last time. I was allowed some private with Jerome's body. I wanted to hit him. I wanted to slap him. I was so frustrated and irritated with him. He'd kept this secret from me, and we were supposed to be best friends forever. My life changed within a matter of seconds. I called Omar back and learned that he had sent a limo to pick me up. I couldn't drive. I had no energy. I was shaking. I was going into complete shock. My friend, my buddy, my hairstylist, my diva was gone!

I signed the papers and returned them to Dr. MacDowden. He said he would contact me in a few days. He told me he needed to speak with Jerome's attorney and get his will. I hugged him and left all my information for him to contact me.

For the first time I didn't like the limo ride. I didn't like anything anymore. Diva never got to see my baby. He never got to hold my baby. He never got to pinch my baby. I was so mad. Tears kept falling down my face.

I got home; Omar was waiting by the door for me. "Baby, I'm so sorry. I know I might not be the one you really want to be next to, but I will stay here if you want me to."

"That would be nice, Omar. I do need you right now. I can't focus. I can't stop crying." I grabbed little Omar and Junior and cried myself to sleep. Omar must have come into the room because when I woke up, both of my babies were in the bed. I was still in my rocking chair. I got up and took a shower. I wanted to wash my tears away.

I grabbed my Bible and started reading scriptures. I didn't know what to read. All I knew was to read until I found what I was looking for. I can recall one day in the shop when a really religious woman was getting a roller set. She told us that when you need the Lord, just call on him, and he will answer.

I did just that. I got on my knees and started praying for Jerome:

> *Dear God, I know Jerome didn't live a righteous life, but please take care of him. I loved him like a brother, even though he wasn't. God, please take my pain away and allow me to cry tears of joy instead of sorrow. God, also can you teach me to forgive but not forget? God, I know I'm not the best at expressing how I feel, but I hope you understand that I speak how I feel at that moment. I want you to teach me the right way to live my life for my family and friends. God, I want you to use me as an example to teach others to live the right way. My eyes are wide open, and my ears are listening. Forgive me if I have sinned. I rebuke the devil away from my life and*

*my family. Show me how to live, God. In Jesus name
I pray. Amen.*

I felt so good after asking God to help me. I wanted Jerome
to go to heaven, but I knew only God could judge him. I got up
and kissed my babies. I walked into the living room and sat next
to Omar.

He hugged me. "Tracee, I have missed this family affection
for a while now. I have realized that you were more to me than
I can ever imagine. I want us to try to work on our marriage.
I will go to any marriage counselor and the pastor to get help.
Baby, I missed you."

I asked Omar to stay with me until the funeral preparations
were done. He was so helpful. I wasn't feeling him like I use to.
I was just glad he was willing to help me. I got everything done.
Jerome had a black marble casket trimmed in white gold. I dressed
him in a white shirt with a purple pin-striped suit. These colors
looked good against his skin. I freshly shaved and cut his beard.

He looked like he was going to the Oscars. Diva was going
to get buried in style. After the funeral was over, I went home to
a big surprise. Jerome's attorney was waiting for me. "Hello, Mr.
Mohavier. How are you?"

"Good. I didn't want you to think that Jerome's funeral was
going to end on a sad note."

"I don't understand what you are talking about."

"Well, Jerome made sure that you and your babies were going
to be taken care of, Tracee, Jerome left all of his money and assets
to you."

"Me?"

"Yes, you. He came into my office about a week before the doctor told him he wasn't going to live. I assumed you knew about it."

"No!"

"Well, he turned everything over to you, and also he stated that you would do what was right with the money."

"Wow!"

"I have all the paperwork ready to go. I just need your signature."

"I'm overwhelmed right now! I'm furious, but what can I do about it? Jerome and I had an agreement about what he should do with the money."

"Oh, he did donate quite a bit to all the charities you told him to and to some other ones also."

"Exactly how much money does he really have?"

"*You* have."

"Yes."

"Well, after cashing out and moving your accounts to how they are prepared to keep making interest, you will have eighty million dollars after probate."

I fainted! Eighty million? *Oh, my god!* Jerome never told me that he had this much money."

"He said this was going to help you start you new life."

"Yes, this will help me start a couple of new lives."

"I can have all the accounts transferred into your name in a week."

"Thank you! Thank you!"

I sat in my room and cried some more. I was really upset with Jerome. He died. He left me eighty million dollars. I didn't get to tell him thank you. I was so angry. I got eighty million dollars to start a new life for my children.

I had some unfinished business with Omar first. *I will say a prayer and hopefully whatever I ask God to help me see, he will see me through it.* I got a pen and paper and wrote down everything I like about Omar. I then wrote what I did not like about Omar. I decided that if I had more good than bad, then I knew what to do from there.

The Bad List:

1. Cheater
2. Abusive
3. Mentally abusive
4. Alcoholic
5. Careless

The Good List:

1. Good listener
2. Good provider
3. Good father
4. Loving
5. Caring
6. Nurturing
7. Rich
8. Sexy
9. Religious

So I had my list, and now it was time to pray again. I knew what I wanted, and Omar was not it anymore. I had given him so many chances to get himself right. Omar wanted to have his cake and eat it, too. I refused to give in to him anymore. He had slept with so many women during our relationship that the trust was gone. I would only deal with him on a parent-to-parent basis. When the morning came, I would tell Omar that there would be no more us. I needed to be by myself and focus on my children. I had lost my best friend.

I woke up to the smell of fresh flowers, which meant Omar was in my home. I wanted to talk to him face-to-face about our relationship.

"Omar, we have had a serious past. I have loved you from a distance. I have loved you close. At the end of the day, you are who you are. I know you will never change and I have accepted that. I refuse to love a man who only loves himself. I'm not selfish, but you are. I know you will cheat on me again. I will not give you the chance to do so again. I'm leaving Florida on a good note and with fat pockets. I will allow you to be in our boys' lives. I wish only the best for you, Omar. I just can't allow you to take me under anymore. I love you so much that it doesn't hurt me to tell you how I feel.

"My bags are about to be packed and shipped, along with the rest of my belongings. I will be here for another two weeks, and then I'm going to live in Atlanta, Georgia. My life will begin a new journey for our kids. I hope you find whatever it was or is that you are looking for in the streets. You never wanted a wife; you wanted a trophy. I have realized what I was, and now it is time to move on for good. Omar, I hope whatever you were looking for that you soon will find it. I asked you before I committed to moving here if you would love me the right way. I stuck it out as long as I could.

"You never changed for the better; you got worse. I knew it was over before little Omar. I wanted a baby from you so bad. I thought that it was me and my ways that kept you in the streets. After a long hard sit-down by myself, I realized it was *you* the entire time. I love you so much, but my mind is made up. I have gone back and forth, and forth and back. Omar, you are very selfish, inconsiderate, childish, untrustworthy, conniving, disrespectful, deceiving, misleading, and most of all, a true *fuck-up*!

I'm leaving!

The End

Printed in the United States
by Baker & Taylor Publisher Services